# Rohendra Queen

The Rohendra Complex, Book 4

## Georgina Makalani

Cover Design by Deranged Doctor Designs

ISBN: 978-0-6453956-9-3

**Also by Georgina Makalani**

The Last Dragon Skin Chronicles
The Legend of Iski Flare
The Magics of Rei-Een
The Mark of Oldra
The Raven Crown

The Rohendra Complex:
The Dragonfly
Sparrow Song
Shimmering Bear
Rohendra Queen

# One

----

Khalia ran around the hearth and then out the door of the cottage. Isla held her breath for a moment, but the child knew the way, and she hadn't fallen down the cliff yet. At six summers old, she was small and agile, with sun-browned skin and long auburn hair. Isla had tried to braid it back out of the way for her, and yet it would work its way free more often than not. Thankfully, the girl hadn't managed to catch it in a tree yet. Her bright blue eyes sparkled as she poked her head back in through the door, and Isla felt the pull of the Rohen within her.

"I thought you were going to visit the Master," Isla said.

"I want Gray first."

"He's out in the forest."

"No, he's not."

Isla felt the Rohen—could use the Rohen, but not as Khalia could. They were still learning what skill the child had. In many ways, she reminded Isla of Beth in that she knew what was happening anywhere and everywhere regardless of where she was. Isla missed Beth. She hoped she would get the chance to see her again and visit the forests of Draroh.

She was enjoying her time back in this forest, in her home, especially with Gray. But it always felt borrowed, as though it could end at any point. She looked back to the face of the child peeking around the door with a small smile on her lips.

"Where is he then?"

"He had to go away."

Isla walked towards the door as Khalia disappeared behind it again, and she listened without watching the child scale down the cliff face to the ground below. A sick feeling settled in her stomach. Gray had arrived in the forest with the Rohen and the child she had come to think of as her own, even though she wasn't.

"You are Mother," the child whispered as Isla landed softly at the base of the cliff.

"Where is Gray?" she asked more firmly. There was no one else about. She looked around the narrow valley for the Master.

"The minister has called him."

"Why wouldn't he say something?"

"He didn't want you to worry."

Isla tried not to sigh. She was worried all the time. "It is nearly time," she said, trying not to sound as defeated as she felt. She looked down at the child, whose blue eyes shone even brighter in the morning light. The sun was only just above the valley. She wondered then when Gray had disappeared. Had she seen him this morning? "Draroh," Isla murmured.

"Can I visit there too?"

"One day."

"You always say that when you aren't sure."

"I am sure," Isla said. "Are you?"

The girl smiled broadly up at Isla and then ran along the length of the valley, past the mound that still filled a large amount of their space. So much of Isla's heart had been lost to it. Even now, she felt the loss when she looked at it. A reminder of what she could lose. Khalia ran out into the trees and was gone from sight.

Isla felt a small pang of worry, as she did every time the child slipped from her sight. But Khalia could look after herself, and the Rohen watched over her more closely than even Isla could. Not that she saw them in the valley, or in the trees. She could feel them, but she had not seen them since they had placed the child in her arms. The forest would look after its own. And Khalia was a child of every forest.

"Is she running from her classes?" the master asked. Isla turned slowly, taking him in, wondering why she hadn't heard him approach. His twisted leg dragged a little behind him. Although it was much improved, it was still deformed, and his limp gave him away as he walked.

"She is looking for Gray."

"How far would she go?" he asked, looking into the trees. Isla wondered then if the child could find a way to Draroh to get to him. She gulped down the growing fear. Before she could take a step, Gray emerged from the trees, Khalia's hand in his.

Isla waited. She understood too well what was to come. She was desperate to ask what had occurred when he'd gone to the minister, and yet she didn't want to know. Gray walked straight to them and wrapped his arms around her. His hand still tight around Khalia's, she joined in the hug. Isla felt the calming nature of the child move through her.

Gray said nothing, but his hold remained, and in that she knew what it meant. Her time here was over. She clung to him tighter.

"Isla," a female voice said. She reluctantly released Gray and looked beyond him at the young blonde woman walking forward. There was a confidence about her that reminded her of Alice, and yet something felt a little uncertain as she stopped, her eyes darting over the valley and the high cliff faces.

"Beth?" Isla asked, moving around Gray. When the woman nodded, Isla wrapped her arms around her. "You got so tall."

"It has been some time," she said.

"Too long. What are you doing here? Aren't we lucky you have come to visit..."

"It is time," Khalia said, and the three of them looked at her.

"When did you learn that?" the master asked, standing back a little.

"I have always known," she said with a shrug and a warm smile. Despite the ache spreading through Isla's chest, that smile warmed her.

"Draroh," Isla said. A word that seemed to have been in her thoughts constantly since she'd woken this morning.

"Not the forest," Beth said.

"It is time to leave the trees," Khalia said, looking around, her little face crinkling sadly for the first time. "But they will never leave us."

"Wise, little one," the Master murmured.

"You can't call me that anymore," Khalia said, her hands on her hips. The old man smiled.

"You aren't that big yet," he said.

"I will be." She looked at Isla, the sadness deepening.

"Time to pack," Gray said, guiding the child back towards the wall. She scaled the stonework with little effort. He watched her climb up, standing beneath her, although Isla knew he wouldn't need to step in and save her. She didn't need them in that way; she never really had.

"Mother," she called from the ledge.

"Coming," Isla called back, trying to clear the lump forming in her throat. "She won't be able to call me that," she said, looking at Gray. His gaze was still on the child.

"She will always call you by your title," Beth said, bowing her head.

Isla climbed up the wall, following the child's path and entering the cottage built into the crevice of the valley. It was small, but theirs. A wide bed against one wall, a narrow one against the other. Cupboards were built into crevices, and a table stood beside the hearth at the back of the space.

Khalia sat on her bed, waiting for Isla, it appeared. Isla looked around the space and back to the child, who patted the bed beside her. Isla smiled. Khalia was more the parent at times than Isla could ever be.

"Mother. Mama," she said, a tear running away. It surprised Isla so much that she pulled the child to her chest and ran a hand over her hair.

"You are more than any of us ever could have hoped for."

"When did you first love me?" she asked, leaning heavily into Isla.

"That is a strange question. When have I not loved you?" Isla whispered. "The first moment I saw you, when you were placed into my arms and Gray closed his arms around us. Before then, when he first showed you to me."

"You will stay with me, at Hendra Central?"

"Always," Isla murmured, pulling her closer.

"You won't be able to call me Khalia," she said.

"I will always use your name," Isla said.

"But not this name."

"You are the only Hendra with more than one name." Isla released the small child in her arms and took her by the shoulder. "You are more than Hendra. You are Rohendra."

The girl nodded slowly and chewed on her lip.

"You will know what is right," Isla assured her. "Now pack your things, little Hendra. It is time to leave the colony."

"The forest looks after its own," she whispered.

"Always."

# Two

S tanding in the office of the Hendra was a surreal feeling. It seemed like only days ago that Isla had been here trying to persuade the previous Hendra to see the error of her ways. At the same time, she was overwhelmed by the years of peace spent in the forest, the idea of the city, and the number of people surrounding her and within the building.

Khalia's hand was tight in hers. The council sat around the table. All were familiar and yet looked older and wearier.

They all looked at the child with wonder and some wariness, particularly Solon, the child's uncle. He waved her forward, presumably to look at her more closely, but she didn't move.

"Come," he demanded.

"I am Hendra," she said, her voice frighteningly similar to her predecessor. "You will not direct me."

"I wish to look over you," he said.

"Then come closer," she said, unmoving, her hand still gripping tight to Isla's.

Isla glanced at the expansive glittering city beyond the windows and wondered if it might have been a good idea to travel here and explore at some point over the last few years. But her focus had been on keeping Khalia safe, and she hadn't wanted to leave the forest.

Solon stood and stepped forward. He was tall and lean. He squatted down before the child and placed a hand on her chin, turning her face. Her blue eyes were intense but didn't glow as they had in the forest. Isla wasn't sure if that was due to her name or the distance from the trees, or if she understood how it would unsettle people.

"You look like her," he muttered.

"You have been looking after my Complex, Uncle," she said, her voice level. She didn't acknowledge the mother who had given her life.

"We have done as we were required to do," he said, straightening up.

"That is all that could be asked of you," she returned.

Ebberah stood then and moved slowly around the table, her long flowing dress taking up more room than the slender woman within would have. Isla wondered how her daughter was doing. She couldn't ask, as no one in the room knew of the child's existence. It had been a long time since she had seen her.

Ebberah bowed low before Hendra.

"How is my moon?" Khalia asked. Hendra asked.

"Still too low in the sky," one of the others murmured.

"Where it is meant to be," Hendra said. "Can we go one day?" she asked, looking up at Isla while tugging on her hand.

"One day," Isla replied.

"You have done your duty," Solon said, sitting back at the table. Isla wondered if he was talking to her.

"Mother's duty will never be done."

"She is not your mother," he snapped.

"She is *the* mother. I don't have to explain that to you or anyone else. As long as I am Hendra, she stays."

Solon bowed his head reluctantly. "We have sought more advisors for you—tutors, carers," he added, looking directly at Isla.

"There is no need for you to trouble yourself," Hendra said. She was a bright girl, advanced beyond her years and yet still a small child. Isla gave her hand a squeeze and then let her go.

"Mother remains," she said, an edge creeping into her voice as she looked back at her. Then she took a breath and stepped up to Gray. "I will introduce you to my tutor, Gray E'anah, and my minister, Beth."

"Beth," Solon repeated, "is hardly older than you. What family does she come from? There has never been a minister position before."

"There has always been a minister," Hendra said, "and Beth is all she needs to be."

The chief of Draroh stood, bowed and stepped forward to look over Beth. Then he reached out and took Gray's hand.

"You are where you were meant to be," he said, then turned back to the group seated around the table. "I have no issue with these advisors."

"She is to lead our world," Solon grumbled.

"And those beyond," Hendra added. "The whole Complex. I understand the responsibilities no matter my age. I have prepared my whole life for this. I have surrounded myself with the best people. You will continue as you have to work for me and the Complex."

"Yes, Hendra," most around the table chorused together—except Solon, who stood, bowed low and stalked from the room.

Beyond the broad door he had left open, an older man in uniform hovered. Isla waved him in.

"General," Isla said, bowing her head to him. "It has been a long time."

He looked to the child rather than to Isla when he nodded, and then somewhat uncertainly at the group. Isla wondered if there had been conversations before their arrival as to what would occur next.

"Has it been difficult?" the child asked.

He blinked and then looked at her as though confused by the question. But he gave a short shake of his head.

"The unrest settled after my birth," she said as though she already knew what had been occurring across the Complex. They might not have talked of it, but the child was Rohendra, and she would be more connected to the universe than Isla could ever understand.

He bowed his head again.

"Did they try to take control?" she asked, looking only at him. He paused before he shook his head again. "I doubt my uncle was as polite as he was just now. We shall talk more. I would like to look around the building."

"Which parts?" he asked.

"All of them. Let us start with the Elite and the pit." Her eyes sparkled when she looked up at Isla, who wondered if it would be the same. "We shall finish with my private residence."

He bowed his head. Without a glance at the council around the table, Hendra took Isla's hand and followed the general to the door.

"We shall meet tomorrow," she said as they left the office. The general ushered her into the lift as the secretaries stood to attention behind their desks. Hendra smiled then as Gray and Beth followed them in.

Solon glared beyond his reflection out over the city he had been so sure was his. There had been no word of the child despite the reassurances that she had survived and would return to the role she was destined for. But unlike any Hendra before her, she had been raised not surrounded by those who would train her appropriately in the Central, but in the forest in the far reaches of the planet.

He had fumed at the idea, but no one would back him in retrieving the child. She was being cared for by someone selected by his sister. Or so the story went. He wasn't sure now who had been so clear about it, but the council had allowed it to happen and gotten on with keeping the Complex ticking over in the meantime. He doubted very much that his sister would have allowed that woman anywhere near her child, but then she had married Alice.

The woman had been seen rarely after the death of Hendra, and although the population had believed her to be caring for their child, it wasn't the case. Nor did she seem to want to. He had tried repeatedly to contact her, but she had refused him. If he were Hendra, that would not have happened.

He sighed and turned back to the large room, one he had made his own within Central. Although he travelled back to his home planet of Arnin often enough, he knew his place was here, ensuring the world was moving as it should.

Victor Sem thought he had more control over Rennet, but in truth the chiefs had very little control over anything. The general had been too careful in ensuring they did as was limited by their power and no more. Not that the others outwardly discussed such things or indicated that they would support him as Hendra—or even tried to rule the Complex as a council in her stead.

Which was what they were doing. Solon ground his teeth, his fists tightening at the idea of the little girl—and she was little. Even for her age, she was small. Maybe they had taught her far more than he'd thought they could. The woman she referred to as Mother had been a wanted criminal not so long ago, and despite his sister's announcement of her pardon, he knew she wouldn't have survived if his sister had.

He sat slowly on the edge of a chair. Reaching forward, he poured water into a cup, surprising himself as it splashed. He was wound too tight; his muscles so tense he was shaking. He had never cared much for his sister; she was older, difficult and too wrapped in what was hers. He sighed, closing his eyes and remembering her sitting across from him on a lounge, surprised by his life and that she didn't know. He had thought at the time just how much of a surprise it was that she had no interest or understanding of his life.

He had married well, produced several children to ensure the continuation of the family line and the control of Arnin. He had always wanted more, no matter what he had told his sister, and she had understood that much of him. But they were family—they were Hendra, even if he was never intended to hold the title. And he had thought to get it, until he had seen the child and the power within. It was as though she had been born for it. No matter who had raised her, she was her mother's daughter.

He would have to find a different way.

A soldier standing just inside the doorway cleared his throat, but Solon didn't look up from the cup. "Where is she?" he asked.

"Taking a tour of the building."

Solon looked up at the soldier, taking in his stance and crisp uniform. He wished he had his own Calder, someone who would do as required with little fuss and little explaining, but he too had disappeared. Too much surrounding his sister's death and the events that led up to it was unexplained.

"What does she think she will learn?"

"She started with the Elite."

"That woman was Elite?" he muttered, looking back at the cup as the water splashed about it. He pushed it over, spilling what was left across the table. The soldier remained motionless. "What do we know of where they were living?"

"Nothing further. We had early intel, but the forest seemed to hamper our attempts to get in."

Solon glared at him. He had heard this before, too many times over the years. "She should have been raised here. The people will question her validity."

"She is the image of her mother," the soldier returned.

"Which one?" Solon spat and stomped back to the window. "I want an audience. First thing tomorrow and on my own, none of her little helpers about."

"I can ask."

"You will make it happen," he demanded, looking across the city and wondering what use a tour of the building would be for a six-year-old. Just what did she think she was going to learn? What did she think she was going to be able to do with it all?

In the lingering silence, he was too aware of the soldier still present in the room. "What else?"

"Chief X'ang would like to see you."

"Now?"

"He still blames the former Hendra for much of the damage to his planet."

"We have discussed this ad nauseam since her death. It is somewhat repaired. It will be for the new Hendra to determine the fate of the mines and perhaps his desiccated planet."

"Sir," the soldier said, and although Solon didn't hear him walk across the room, he heard the swish of the door as it opened and closed behind him.

They didn't want him as Hendra. As a council, they wouldn't support anyone from within the ranks moving forward, despite Ebberah's actions in the lead-up to his sister's death. And yet they expected him to answer for the mistakes that had been made. If they were mistakes. He had no idea why his sister would have tried to destroy the mines, other than she had deemed them illegal. He hoped that in her attempt to do so, she hadn't been aware of the damage to the planet it might have caused.

He sighed and leaned forward into the cool glass. There was no way to know what she'd been thinking. She would have told no one, other than Calder perhaps, and that was a mystery they would never solve. X'ang could take it up with the new Hendra. He was curious to see what the child would say.

Solon tried not to look disappointed as he stood in the middle of Hendra's office the following morning. She had accepted his request to see her, and now she sat on the floor of the office, her back against the desk while her fingers worked through the thick rug. He hadn't been granted a private audience, as he had hoped when he first entered the room. The three carers who had arrived with her sat at the large table, two reading old books. The woman, the Mother—although he was loathe to call her that—was watching too closely.

He cleared his throat, and Hendra looked up at him with the bluest eyes he had ever seen. They were not her mother's eyes, yet there was something familiar in them.

"Please sit, Uncle. You are so tall."

He bowed his head and took a step closer before sitting awkwardly on the floor in front of her. He might have done this with his own children on occasion, but only rarely, and he didn't remember it being so difficult to bend his legs.

"What would you like to talk about?" she asked, her blue eyes focused only on him. "I would guess your planet, but you have so many questions."

He bowed his head. "Do you have plans for my planet?"

She shrugged, her head cocked a little to the side as though asking what he thought those plans might be and what she thought they might need to be. He sighed and then straightened his back.

"Urgway," she said as though reading his mind. "Interesting that you would want to know about another planet, and one that you have little time for."

He opened his mouth and then closed it, glancing over his shoulder at those behind, two still reading and the woman watching.

"Why would I ask you about Urgway?"

"Because you wish to know what Hendra did there, why she did as she did. What it might mean for you."

He shook his head once, and she smiled. She looked far more childlike than before that it unnerved him. She knew far more than she should—far more than a child her age should know.

She lifted her hands from the carpet and folded them in her lap. "The mines will reopen. The planet will be healed."

"Healed?" he asked quickly.

"Would you see it stay as it is?"

He shook his head, unsure exactly what her words meant. His carefully crafted questions had escaped him, and he had no idea what he was doing in the room.

"Would you like to go home?" she asked, and again he shook his head. She smiled again. "Your family would miss you, but I could use your counsel."

He bowed his head to her. "Thank you, Hendra."

"Tell me of your forests," she said, moving up onto her knees and leaning forward. A glint in her eye made him take a second look.

"Forests?"

"Tall trees," she said, raising her hand above her head. "Lots of them, together."

"On Arnin?"

"Yes," she said more firmly, something a little frightening in the way she said it.

"I don't visit them as I should."

"Why?" she asked just as a child would, with no understanding of why he wouldn't want to walk through the trees.

"I don't care for trees."

She stood quickly enough to make him sit back. But her eyes were on the woman behind him, and she rushed forward into her arms. The woman hadn't moved from the chair and closed her arms around Hendra, the child appearing as small as she was when she pushed her face into the woman's chest. The woman ran her hand down Hendra's fine hair and whispered something in her ear.

Gray E'anah, the tutor, closed his book and stood. They could have been mistaken for a family unit at that point. The young woman—the minister, although Solon was still to learn exactly what that was—closed her eyes.

"I am sorry to have upset you," he said slowly as he climbed to his feet. "We could visit the trees together. I understand that you have grown in the forests of Rennet, but we do not all have such opportunity."

The child turned slowly, still in the woman's arms. She looked him over as though trying to read him again. Then she turned her face away.

"I think that will do for today," Tutor E'anah said.

"There will be more taxing topics to discuss than trees," Solon said. The woman scowled. "She will need to learn her place."

"I know what I am," Hendra whispered. "You should learn your place in the Complex."

He was surprised by the words, but they weren't said unkindly. His sister would have sliced him with her tongue. He bowed his head, and the door was already opened for him before he reached it. Although he wasn't sure how, as there was no one on the other side when he walked out into the foyer. The door was quick to close behind him. That hadn't gone as he had hoped.

# Three

I sla's heart ached. She leaned back on the bed, too large and too soft, and
missed her little cottage built into the crevices of the valley. Khalia slept
in her arms. The child's small body pressed against her, head on her chest,
breath slow and steady.

"This is harder than I imagined," Gray whispered beside her, a book in
his hand and his focus on the child.

"She knows so much and yet is still so young. Will it get easier?" Isla
asked.

"I don't know. It is day two, and we started with her uncle and his lack
of understanding of the world. She doesn't understand them."

"I don't understand them," Isla added.

He smiled then and leant in to kiss her lips. "When do you think she'll
start sleeping in her own bed?" he murmured as they pulled apart, looking
across the room at the narrow bed against the wall.

"We could push her to the end and wouldn't even notice she was here.
This bed is huge," Isla murmured, but she continued to hold the child tight.
Gray had lifted her gently earlier and placed her in her own bed, but she had
lasted less than a minute before she'd rolled out, padded across the room
and climbed between them. "She is scared," Isla said. But was she as scared
as she should be for a child her age in this situation, or was it more for Isla's

benefit? Isla was far more afraid for the child now than she had ever been in the colony.

"I thought Ebberah would ask for a meeting," he said.

"I think they want to give her some time, and then the asking—or demanding—will begin."

"Will they really ask for so much?"

"They have had control for the last six years. I'm not sure they are going to be willing to give it up."

"X'ang was quick to trust."

"We'll see. He wants her there to oversee the mines, to prove that she means what she says."

Gray shuffled closer and wrapped his arm around the two of them. "I don't like that idea."

"Maybe we can visit the forests there and that will help."

"Help who?" he asked, his breath tickling her cheek.

"Me. I miss them. Maybe Solon should come to see what she can do," she whispered, turning towards him and pressing her lips to his.

"That sounds like inviting trouble," he replied.

"I'm tired," a soft voice whispered. Khalia wiggled out from between them, crawled across the expanse of the bed, padded across to her own and snuggled in quickly.

Isla rolled to watch her for a moment, and it appeared she had slipped easily back into sleep. Gray wrapped around Isla, his hold tight as though she might slip away, but his kisses on her neck were soft and gentle.

It felt like an age since Isla had been inside a ship. The silver one they travelled in reminded her of someone lost long ago. As they flew above the crimson sand of Urgway, Isla wondered for the first time why there wasn't something special for the Hendra in terms of a vessel. Surely the previous Hendra had something she used? But she had rarely travelled.

"Why are we travelling this way?" Khalia asked, leaning in close.

"It is how most people travel and what is expected."

The child nodded, looking across at those opposite her. Gray's gaze was focused on her. Beth sat with her eyes closed, hands gripping the harness holding her into the seat. Her face was pale, and several times Gray had whispered encouraging words to her throughout the journey. Perhaps it would have been easier if they had travelled via the Rohen and met the others on Urgway. Isla wasn't sure it was a good idea to allow these people to see just what skills Khalia had, and Beth agreed.

Solon sat further away, looking through the small windows out across the sand. He had said nothing for the entire journey, and Isla worried he had more planned than he was giving away.

As the ship landed and the door opened, Beth appeared to breathe for the first time. She unbuckled quickly, almost leaping from the ship out onto the tarmac. The sound of construction work echoed across the sand. The sun was bright, and she lifted her arm up as Gray dropped a cape across her head and shoulders. Isla held Khalia back, although it was hard.

"Remember what we said about the sun?" she reminded the child.

Khalia nodded, the tension in her arm evident as she took Isla's hand. "We will see them, won't we?"

"That isn't up to me," Isla said. The Rohendra had not visited despite Isla's awareness of their presence in Khalia's life. She was sure the child spoke with them more than even Beth did.

"You want to go into the mine?" Solon asked, coming to stand beside her as several men erected a covered walkway from the ship across the tarmac.

"Don't you?" Khalia asked, a sparkle in her eye as she turned and leapt from the doorway into Gray's waiting arms, not waiting for her uncle to respond.

"I'm not sure it is safe," Solon mumbled.

"And yet you asked the Hendra here," Isla said.

He looked at her then as though only just remembering she was there. He took a deep breath and nodded once. "I need her to see what the world is."

"Despite her age," Isla said, moving towards the door as the others walked along the covered walkway, "she understands far more than either of us."

"Truly?" he asked, pulling her to a stop with a hand on her arm.

Gray had stopped a bit ahead, pointing out across the landscape for both Beth and Khalia. He picked her up so she could follow the line of his finger, her arms tight around his neck. How long could this continue?

"Mother?"

Isla turned then and took in the tall man studying her.

"That is your title?"

She bowed her head. "You can call me Isla."

"Isla, what do you think I am trying to do here?"

"I'm not sure, but you might find the child is far more than she appears to be."

Isla strode across the tarmac to join the others, feeling his eyes on her back. She needed him to understand just what the child was without actually telling him. How would the Complex accept a child of the Rohendra?

Buildings were going up around the opening of the mine. Although Isla was sure the ground had been split open the last time she was here, it was solid now. The tall structure that had stood above the opening was back in place. She looked into the darkness beyond. She knew the child would be safe, and yet something niggled at her. A miner appeared at the opening, his old clothing worn and grubby. She wondered what they had done over the years since the mines had been destroyed—or were they already working them again and this was all for show?

"You should wear something protective," he said. "The fumes are still something to be wary of."

Isla nodded, and masks were handed out. Khalia looked somewhat uncertain, but Isla helped her to fit hers. The mask was small but not designed for a child. "It is all for show," Isla whispered, running her hand over it and changing the shape so that it fit snuggly against the girl's face.

"We've set up torches along the main tunnel," the miner said.

She nodded thanks as she stood and took the child's hand. He headed into the lift shaft, Solon striding in after him. Isla was reminded that his sister would never have come willingly to see what lay beneath the surface of the planet, even if she wanted it all for herself.

Beth and Gray followed him in. Isla wondered then at the lack of security, the lack of soldiers. Were they not as interested in keeping the child safe? She heard running and turned to see the general racing towards them across the tarmac, surprisingly energetic for a man his age. He must have been in one of the buildings dotted around the space.

He bowed low to Khalia and then smiled for Isla. "We are struggling somewhat with the communications out here. Where are the others?" he asked, looking around.

"What others?" Khalia asked as the lift creaked and then started a slow descent.

"Soldiers?" he clarified.

"I was just thinking the same, but we haven't seen any. I assumed they would be here."

"I sent Elite to watch over her on the journey."

Solon grinned as he was lost to the dark.

"It is safe," Khalia said, reaching out and taking the general's hand, and then they were pulled from the hot surface of the planet to the cool, dark tunnel below.

Isla adjusted easily to the dim light.

"It is safe," Khalia repeated.

"How in the name of the stars did you do that?" the general stammered, stepping back as Khalia released her hold on him.

"You have travelled that way before," Isla said.

He blew out a slow breath and shook his head. Either he didn't want to remember what had occurred when he had been face-to-face with the Rohen or he didn't actually remember. Isla put her arm around Khalia's shoulder and pulled her closer as the general cleared his throat and shook out his arms. Khalia wrapped her arms tight around Isla as the general fell to his knees and bowed low before her.

"Don't do that," she whispered, her face buried against Isla.

"You are something very special," he said.

"She is something that needs protecting," Isla said.

The general nodded and climbed to his feet, appearing older as he did so. "Do we wait for the others?"

"I want to see the trees," Khalia murmured, her face still buried. She sounded more like the small child she was than the leader they wanted her to be.

"We can try," Isla offered, taking her hand. They started along the tunnel, the general close behind.

"Trees?" he asked.

Isla looked down at Khalia, wondering if this was a good idea, but she said nothing as the girl moved ahead of Isla and pulled at her to move faster. Then she stopped, holding out her hand to the general once more. He stepped up and took it without hesitation, although Isla noted he squeezed his eyes closed tightly as though afraid of what might come next.

Isla breathed in the scent of the forest, familiar and safe, as Khalia let go of her hand and raced forward. Isla wasn't worried for her among the trees. They were home, if a different home, and the Rohen would ensure she was safe. There were some boulders scattered about the floor as though someone had thrown them. She looked up at the gentle glow of the cavern's ceiling, which appeared just as it always had, and was sure the Rohen had fixed it.

The general made a noise of wonder, and she looked up at the trees glowing blue. The wonder was reminiscent of when Gray had said the forest's name, but this was more intense, brighter. She searched amongst the trees for a sign of Khalia. When she couldn't find the girl, she raced forward. The general was close behind. It wasn't that she feared, but she had to see her.

Khalia stood with her hands against the trunk of a tree, her forehead resting against it. Although Isla couldn't hear what she was saying, her lips moved quickly and silently.

Isla had never heard her speak the words. She understood that Khalia spoke Rohendra, or at least understood it. She was Rohendra, after all. That was something Isla had always been aware of, but it wasn't until this instant that she fully understood just what it meant.

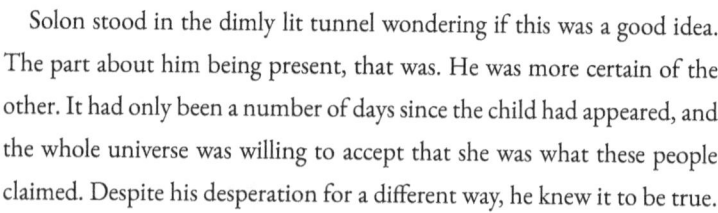

Solon stood in the dimly lit tunnel wondering if this was a good idea. The part about him being present, that was. He was more certain of the other. It had only been a number of days since the child had appeared, and the whole universe was willing to accept that she was what these people claimed. Despite his desperation for a different way, he knew it to be true.

But he wasn't going to support a child in the role he should have. The one he'd nearly had over the last six years waiting for that child to appear.

She unsettled him, if he was honest. She was so childlike, reminding him of his youngest daughter in too many ways, and yet she was something else entirely. She was confident, able to converse and argue in a manner well beyond her years. In fact, with much of what he had heard from her, she was more advanced in intellect and understanding of the universe than many of the chiefs.

He had expected Ebberah to protest more. Yet she hadn't, and X'ang had been only too happy to accept the child on Urgway. A planet that had nearly been destroyed by the actions of his sister, and Solon was yet to fully understand how it had been repaired to the degree it had. The people had talked of how the planet had nearly been blown apart, how great craters and crevices had appeared across the surface, swallowing whole towns. But there had been no such evidence when they'd flown over it. He wondered if he would be able to create an accident or illness down here after all.

They had waited far too long in the tunnel, and the lift had yet to reappear. "Is she afraid, do you think?"

"Who?" Gray asked, looking along the walls in the dim light.

"The child."

"Hendra," the large man corrected, although Solon had yet to hear anyone in her little party call her that. He had heard her call the soldier *Mama*, which had caused him more pain than he'd expected the word could create. His sister would likely not have allowed such a familiar term to be used either way, but this woman was not the Hendra's mother.

"Hendra," he muttered, looking along the tunnel and then back to the lift shaft. "Why isn't she coming?"

"They are already here," said the minister, another child.

"Excuse me?"

"In the trees?" Gray asked.

She nodded, a small smile spreading across her lips. "Shall we join them?"

Gray looked to Solon, and the smile disappeared.

"We could leave him behind," the child offered.

"I wouldn't mind that. But then I expect he is keen to return to the surface to claim the Hendra missing and that he will rule in her stead."

"I would never," Solon said, trying to sound hurt by the idea, his hand to his chest. But it did seem like an easy fix. "What trees?" he asked.

Something silver caught the dim light, and the child nodded as she stepped forward. Solon was distracted. Was there a leak? Should he have considered more protection from the gasses of the Rohen and the possible risks inside the mine? He was surprised no one had said anything about the lack of soldiers. And then the world darkened around him.

Someone had hold of his sleeve. He was wondering if he had made a terrible mistake when the light increased around him. He stood amidst a blue forest, the trees glowing unnaturally. Was he losing his mind?

"General," Gray said. Solon stepped back from the odd sight before him.

"Tutor E'anah, I should not be surprised to see you here."

"And yet you appear to be."

"I am somewhat surprised by it all, let alone what our Hendra is."

"Where is Hendra?" Solon asked, finding his voice and looking around. Isla appeared from between the trees. "Why is he here?"

"It is time," the minister murmured, and although the older woman glared at him, she nodded slowly.

"Where is the Hendra?" Solon repeated, more forcefully this time. A fear covered his skin that he had been led here to be trapped, and he wasn't even sure where here was.

"I am here, Uncle." The child appeared beside Isla, her hand slipping too easily into the woman's, and sighed contentedly.

"Where are we?" Solon asked, looking around, but he couldn't make out anything other than the odd trees.

"Beneath Urgway's surface," Isla said.

"I haven't seen them glow like this," Gray said, stepping forward to put his palm flat against the closest tree.

Isla looked down at the child, and the man smiled as though a proud father.

"You are not family," Solon growled.

"Not as you might understand the term, but we are all connected, some of us more so than others." The child released her hold on the woman's hand and stepped towards Solon, reaching out to touch Gray as she passed him. He gave her a nod.

"Explain it to me," Solon demanded.

"It is not something that you would understand. You don't hold the same connection. No matter how I tried to show you the Rohendra, you would not see them."

The general opened and then closed his mouth as though to say something and then changed his mind. "You have seen, General," Hendra said without looking at him. Solon felt his uneasiness growing. "You understand. Although you do not share it, you know what it is to be part of the Rohendra Complex."

"I understand!" Solon snapped, stepping forward to meet the child walking towards him. She raised her hand, and he followed the movement, looking beyond the trees towards a sky that wasn't there. A stone ceiling reflected the odd light. Just as he was wondering again at the trees, the light dimmed and other plants around the cavern glowed different colours. Fungi in greens, reds and yellows dotted the rock, changing the view of the world completely.

He looked at the child, her eyes closed to the wonder she was pointing out as her lips moved silently, and he wondered if this was her doing. Was there a possibility that the connection the child talked of was far more than he could understand?

"Your father would not have told you as you would not have believed, just as Hendra did not."

"You are Hendra," he said, although he understood whom she spoke of. He wondered at the child not referring to her as mother.

"I am also Khalia." Her eyes were a brilliant blue in the dim light, to the point he almost thought they shone with the same magic as the trees.

"I don't understand," he said, looking at the child as though for the first time. "You are Hendra. You can only be Hendra."

She shook her head.

"Khalia," he repeated, her eyes glowing that bit brighter. The trees appeared to lean in around her. "Everlasting," he murmured.

She smiled at him then, her head tilting a little to the side as she studied him with those odd eyes. "You might be more than I thought, Uncle."

"This does not explain what is happening here. What has happened to Urgway? How was it repaired? Why are we in a forest?" He had far more questions, but the smile on the child's face drew him to stop. There was something there he would never fully understand, just as she had claimed. No matter how she explained it to him, he would never know.

"Why bring me here?" he asked, crossing his arms. If he wasn't to understand, why bother including him in the conversation?

"It is time for you to meet the rest of the family," she said.

"Family?" He took a hurried step back, tripping over something on the ground and falling back against a tree. Someone else had walked from between the trees, but it was not like anyone he had seen before. The creature, for that was all he could call it, was taller than a man but shaped like one. Its featureless face, like the rest of it, was made of solid metal.

"The Rohendra," the child said, as though it were the most natural thing in the world. The general looked a little unsteady, but the others in the group didn't appear to even flinch at the sight of the creature.

"You may know them as Rohen," Isla said.

"Rohen," he stammered, and a sudden understanding of his sister's need to destroy the mines washed over him. "They are using you to control the Complex," he breathed.

"They are the Complex," Hendra said, as though he were a fool. "The Hendra is to work with them to ensure the Complex continues in prosperity. That was nearly ended. The Complex was nearly ended. I am putting it right."

"How?" he stammered.

"You are here for other reasons," the creature before him appeared to say. Although its face didn't move at all, the sound vibrated through him.

"Other than what?" Solon asked. "I'm not even sure where we are or why the Hendra brought me here."

"You want control of what is not yours."

Solon shook his head, but that had been his plan. That was what he had wanted. Was it possible that he had no real idea of what the Complex was at all?

The creature tilted its head forward as though in agreement, and he wondered if it could read his mind.

"They understand far more than you." Hendra stepped forward, reaching out, and the creature took her hand. What had appeared as nondescript were now clearly defined fingers that laced through hers. She gave another contented sigh. "We are connected. We are Rohendra, and together we are the Rohendra Complex."

Solon's legs gave way beneath him, and he slipped to the ground.

"You are scaring him," Isla said, stepping forward and placing her hand on Khalia's shoulder. "He doesn't understand."

The man leaning back against the tree, his legs sprawled out before him, shook his head and then nodded quickly in agreement.

"It is hard to fathom and yet makes perfect sense," the general murmured, and the man looked up at him as though he were crazy. "I've seen them before, when I was with the former Hendra, when she was trying to destroy this and nearly destroyed us all."

"She wouldn't do that," Solon stammered.

"Of course she would. She wasn't willing to share. You are very alike," the little minister said.

"Were you even alive then?" he snapped.

"I saw what was to come."

"But it wasn't destroyed," he said, looking around.

"It has been protected and repaired," the Rohen hummed, and Isla realised just how much she had missed the sensation. She had felt the Rohen around her, but the direct communication had been something else.

"What do you think I can do with this knowledge? The universe won't believe me. No one would believe me."

"We don't need anyone to believe you," Hendra said. "We need you to understand so that I can do as I need to as Hendra."

Solon shook his head, and Isla wondered if he disagreed with Khalia being Hendra or if he would support her.

"The other chiefs?" he stammered.

"They understand. Ebberah has seen what the world is, as has Draroh's chief. Chief X'ang works with the Rohendra to repair his planet. I am sure Sem has always understood what the world is; he senses more than he has let on."

"I have been alone," Solon said. The idea appeared to cause him pain. Isla wondered at the brother of the former Hendra, always being near the top and yet never achieving it.

"In your ignorance?" Khalia said, the words a genuine query as to his concern, but his face hardened. "No," she said. "There are many who do not understand and do not see the world for what it is. But now you do."

"And yet you don't believe that I will truly understand it."

She nodded slowly as the scowl remained fixed to her uncle's face.

"You are needed to support the Hendra," the Rohen said.

"How do you expect me to do that?"

"As you would have your sister," the Rohen continued.

"And yet I wonder if you understand what I would have done to take control from her."

"It was not something you could do, nor can you now. Hendra is the Complex. She holds it together. Khalia will hold the Complex in balance."

"For how long?" he asked, the same cruel grin Isla had glimpsed earlier returning.

"It will be everlasting," the Rohen hummed.

The man's face turned contemplative. "Will she hold it together forever, or will her efforts be all that is needed?"

There was no response. Isla wondered the same thing. She knew Khalia was something very different, and yet she still thought of her as a child—as her child. The silver being turned towards her, and she tried not to sigh. She wasn't the mother; she was the one chosen to watch over the girl and ensure she was as she should be.

"That is the role of a mother," the silver Rohen rumbled through her. As she felt the relief of the words, tears prickling behind her eyes, Gray's arm closed around her. Khalia had somehow managed to squeeze between them.

"Don't fear," she whispered as Beth said the same words.

"There is more," Solon said. Isla looked at Beth, who gave the smallest shake of her head. Not that Isla would tell him anything further. It was for Khalia to determine what information he needed to be of use.

"Why don't you question more?" Solon suddenly snapped, raising his finger accusingly towards the general.

"I know my place in the world, and that is to keep the Hendra safe."

"There seem to be many acting at that," Solon mumbled.

"And yet you still manage to derail Elite from watching over her."

"I have more sway than you would like."

"No more," the general muttered.

"I am part of this now!"

"You are in on the power behind the Complex—you are in on the aim of the Rohendra to ensure balance. You are to ensure you do as required to keep your planet in balance and the Complex at peace."

"You mean I might upset them?" Solon laughed, his voice stilling as he looked to the tall silver being before him. "I would not aim to."

"Your wife is strong, your daughter more so," the Rohen hummed.

"Are you threatening me?" Solon stepped forward, his slender body appearing closer to the Rohen.

"I am reminding you of your obligation."

"You don't need to. My family has led this Complex for generations, since the beginning of time."

The creature remained unmoving.

"I know what I am."

"Your sister thought she knew," Gray whispered. "And then she learnt the truth. You are learning in a different way, so that you might take the time to understand."

"She learnt her place," the Rohen said. "Despite her best efforts to try to teach us."

"Did she try such a thing?" Solon asked.

"She did."

"That is why she disappeared."

"To protect the Complex, she had to step back and allow our queen to step up."

"Queen?" Solon asked, taking in the child still pressed against Isla.

Isla found herself nodding. She still wasn't quite sure at times what Khalia was, but she was far more to the Complex than Hendra. Isla smiled at the child, feeling contented as the trees grew brighter. She squinted as the sharp blue glow increased to a point that she could hardly see. Solon lunged forward, pulling Khalia from Isla's grasp, and the Rohen growled an odd noise that echoed from the cavern walls.

The Rohen staggered as though injured and then melted into the ground. The trees dimmed. Isla grabbed at Gray, his arm still around her.

"Khalia," she screamed into the dark. "Khalia!"

There was no response, and Gray whispered a word she would never learn. The trees glowed a little brighter, but not as they had in Khalia's presence. Isla searched wildly for a sign of the child amongst the trees. She pulled from Gray's arms, moving between the trees, but there was no sign of the girl anywhere.

She searched out Beth, standing still and silent, her eyes closed. Isla reached for her but was too scared to touch her.

"Gone," she whispered, "lost."

"No, no, no," Isla insisted. The child had not been out of her sight or hearing since she was a baby. Even when they'd searched the forests around the colony, Isla was never far behind, watching just in case the child needed her. She had allowed the other children more freedoms, but there was something that ached inside her when Khalia was away from her.

"He won't hurt her," the general said, his face pale.

"You don't know that. He just told us how he plotted to remove his sister. No one has ever removed a Hendra."

"And he did not manage to defeat her," the general said, his voice level. "The Rohendra will protect her."

"I don't think they can," Beth whispered, her eyes still closed. "Can you feel them?"

Isla closed her own eyes and stretched out her senses. She could feel the Rohen in the world surrounding them, working through the planet. But there was something else, something she didn't quite understand, as though the hum of the universe had changed.

# Four

Kalli sat back against the smooth wooden wall and breathed in the hum of the universe. His connection with the world grew every day, and in many ways he could use the Rohen as they had used him so long ago. He wasn't bitter, but he was annoyed they had allowed him to be taken from the world at such a time, hidden away so far from those he wanted to be with. His child being one of them.

He'd known she was his the instant Gray had said her name and she'd appeared as a shimmering woman before Hendra. There had been more of him involved in creating the child than anyone would allow him to claim.

She was his. She was him.

Although now she appeared as a frightened child, her brilliant blue eyes wide as she stood on the opposite side of the room and stared at him.

"I won't hurt you." He kept his voice low and his body still despite wanting desperately to leap to his feet, cross the room and wrap her in his arms.

"You already have."

He shook his head.

"You have taken me from Mama."

"Your mother…" He wanted to explain that her mother was gone. He wondered at her upbringing so far, how she had lived amongst the other children, her relationship with Alice and the stories Gray might have read to her. He wondered why he hadn't been told anything of her time there.

"*The* mother," she said, her voice surprisingly level. "She was destined for me as I was for her. You know her as Island Tarle. You are not what you want to be."

He turned his head a little to the side, wondering at the strength behind her words. "Isla," he mused. Odd that she would have stepped in to raise the child. "What do you think I want to be?"

"A father," she said. "I know what you are and who you were. I am glad she was able to save you."

"Isla? She did no such thing. It was others who stepped in and saved me as I saved her from your mother."

"There is only one mother, and that is Island Tarle," she repeated, her voice level and firm as though he didn't understand her. "Gray is more father to me than you could ever be. And it was the Rohendra who allowed me to form inside the Hendra, not you."

He opened his mouth and then closed it.

She crossed her arms. It would have been more serious in someone older, but she was still a small child, and the action made him smile.

"I know what you are to me," he said.

"It is what you hope I am," she replied. "You can't keep me here."

"You are the Rohendra queen. I shouldn't imagine I could make you do anything you did not want to do. But there are those who would know you, including me, and those who would use you, such as Isla."

She shook her head. "I have seen what she is and what she will be, as well as what she was."

What skill did this child have that he wasn't aware of? Had he too been lied to?

"Mama is safety itself."

"An interesting idea."

"You will see for yourself."

"Is this something your minister has told you?"

"No," she whispered, closing her eyes. "It is what I know." She sighed rather dramatically and then walked through the wall as though it weren't there. Kalli clambered to his feet and went after her. As he reached the wall, he put his hand to it, opening a panel to reveal an open room that looked out over a forest.

He had found it harder to leave the trees than he had first thought possible, but the feel of the Rohen—the hum of what he knew to be the heartbeat of the universe—was stronger in the forests. Since he had returned to the Complex, he had visited most of the forests in some form or another. When he had asked for Solon and the child to be carried to him, it had been done without question.

The child now stood at the window looking over the trees. He wondered if she could walk through the window into the forest and then back to Isla, just as Isla had done so many times. Was that a skill she could teach, or was this child—his child—so much more than one with the Rohen?

Watching her from behind, her hands pressed against the glass, he realised she wasn't aware of all aspects of the Rohen or he would not have been able to act as he had.

"Where is my uncle?"

"Do you miss him?"

She remained still and quiet.

Kalli sighed. This was not going as he had hoped it would. "He is elsewhere."

"He did not know that you could do this," she said. It wasn't a question.

"He doesn't even know I'm alive."

"That was a clever trick," she whispered against the glass.

"Thank you."

"It was not a compliment," she said, not turning from the trees. "Nor is it yours to take. You were saved by another—you didn't ask for it, although you may have asked for this." She turned slowly, taking him in with those brilliant eyes. *Did they glow?*

"You are Rohendra," he breathed.

"Yes," she said, bowing her head. "I am Hendra, and yet only because I was conceived within the previous Hendra. I am and yet not her child. I am their child. I am Island's child."

"You sound confused as to your origins," he muttered, although she seemed fairly certain for a child of her age. Her eyes glowed a little brighter. Despite Isla having only been involved in the raising of the child, he saw much of her standing before him. "You are mine," he said, more to convince himself, and yet he had told Hendra herself that he knew the child to be Rohendra at the start of this.

"I am not yours." She lifted her chin. Her defiance at the idea made him shudder. He had only thought of her for so long, and yet she was rejecting him without knowing him. Again, he could only think of Isla.

Her lips moved as though she were speaking, but he couldn't hear her. He took a step closer. She flinched at the movement, the first sign of fear. He stopped.

"What is it?" he asked. "What do you need?"

She shook her head, her lips still moving, and a strange hum covered his skin. Then she was gone. He sucked in a breath, racing forward to where she had been. She shouldn't be able to do that. He had asked, and she had been given, and no one could take her again.

The odd feeling around Isla increased. She was desperate to leave the trees in search of Khalia, but she wasn't sure she could reach her. And then the child was wrapped around her middle once more. She breathed out the breath she hadn't realised she had been holding, and dropped to her knees to wrap her arms around the girl.

"Something is wrong," Khalia whispered.

"Where did you go? How did Solon do that?"

"He didn't," Beth answered for her, standing with her hands clenched at her sides.

"What did you see?" Isla asked, standing slowly and pulling the child up into her arms. She would never let her go again.

Beth shook her head, scrunching her eyes closed as though trying to see something she couldn't understand.

"Where were you?" she asked Khalia again when Beth didn't respond.

The child squeezed her arms tight around Isla's neck and leaned her head on her shoulder. Her breath was warm on Isla's neck, and the feeling helped ground her. "Kalli," she whispered.

It was as though the world had stopped. He had been lost twice to her now. Her gaze found Gray studying her from across the space. It was only then that she noticed the trees glowed brighter now that the child was here.

"He is gone," Isla whispered, lost as to how she could process such news.

"There is something wrong," Khalia breathed against her neck.

"With the Rohendra?" Isla asked. Beth sucked in a deep breath.

"They are one; they are many," Beth said.

"They are more than one," Khalia said.

"I don't understand," Isla admitted.

"No," Khalia said, her little arms holding tighter. "I want to go home."

"Of course," the general murmured, stepping forward. "I will have the ships readied and we will return to Central."

"No," she said, lifting her head. "I want to go home."

"Will we find what we need there?" Beth asked.

"We are in the trees," Gray murmured, taking the child from Isla's arms. She wanted to scream for him to stop. "We are safe in the trees."

"Not these trees," Khalia said, reaching for the nearest one. They stood together, the child in his arms with her arm around his neck. Her other palm pressed into a tree, and he did the same.

"What is happening?" the general asked as the trees around them faded.

"Not all of the Rohendra work together," Khalia said.

"How can that be?" Isla asked.

She shook her head, her hand still pressed into the bark of the tree. Gray had closed his eyes as though reading the very same bark. "I don't know. I have not felt it. I still don't feel it."

"And yet you know it to be true," Isla returned. The bright blue eyes of the child focused on her. She understood that. The hum had changed. Something wasn't right with the Complex, but she didn't understand what that was or what could be done to fix it. There was no clear issue, no enemy standing before them. "Why Kalli?"

"He wanted me to stay with him."

Gray's arm closed tighter around the child as she leaned into him, planting a soft kiss on the side of his head. He lifted his other arm around her.

"I understand what I am," she said, her little voice lifting through the trees as though the leaves carried her voice.

"You are a child of the Rohendra," Gray answered.

"And yours," she said, pressing her face against his again.

"Is Solon involved?"

"No, he wasn't there. I fear Kalli thinks he can be used, that the Rohendra working with him feel he can be used. But I don't understand what they want."

"Beth?" Isla asked, knowing that the young woman had more of a connection than she did to the hum of the universe. But Beth just shook her head.

Isla searched the trees for a sign of the Rohen. They had been with them not long ago, and yet there was nothing of them now besides the trees. Which of them would tell her the truth of what the world was? Why had she not understood this sooner? Had the decision just been made, or was it something else? A greater plan.

"They saw her as Queen," she breathed. "The Rohendra knew the outcome of the fight long before it happened. They needed us in place."

Gray nodded, his arms still tight around Khalia. Her little face was pressed against his, her arms tight around his neck. "Where do we go?" he asked.

"Home," Khalia whispered.

"General," Isla said, looking at the man studying the child. "I will ask you to investigate Chief Solon, see if he is at home or elsewhere and what he might know of what happened today. Get an understanding of what he thinks might happen."

The general saluted her, which made her flinch. He turned and then turned back to her. Isla stepped forward and touched his arm, sending him back to the surface without her. She wasn't leaving Khalia again. Her heart still beat too fast at the idea of losing the child.

The remaining group stood together, their arms around each other reaching for what they didn't understand, and it was Khalia who moved them through the Rohen. But as Isla blinked up into the sun-dappled trees, she had no real understanding of where she was. It wasn't Rennet—it wasn't her forest. It wasn't a place she had thought Khalia would understand to be home.

"Where are we?" Beth asked, stepping back from the group and leaning into a tall, broad tree.

Isla breathed in the world around her, the familiar grounding scent of trees, of forest. The leaf litter, the sound of the wind moving through the leaves, it was both familiar and foreign.

"Home," Khalia breathed once more as Gray lowered her to the ground. She moved quickly between the trees. Isla made to follow, the same fear as when the girl had disappeared from the cavern gripping her heart, but Gray held her back.

"I can't lose her," she whispered.

"You won't," he returned, his voice just as quiet as he pulled her close. "Not here."

"I don't know where we are."

"I have seen it in my reading, long ago, when I started."

Beth shook her head, and then her body grew still. "We are at the core of it."

"The core of what?" Isla asked.

"Of the universe," Beth whispered. "I didn't think that a place truly existed."

"Akela," Khalia whispered, reappearing, and it was as though the hum of the universe picked up around her. Isla realised she had never felt more alive and secure in her life. "It does not matter where it is. It is here," she said.

Isla licked at her lip and bit down on it. She had been going to ask that very question. But then, she knew it was somewhere she had never been before. Somewhere she would never fully understand. Somewhere outside of the five planets of the Rohendra Complex and yet right in the middle of it.

"Can they explain?" she asked, not that she needed an explanation. "Will they come?"

"They are already here," Khalia said.

Isla glanced around the trees surrounding them and could see no hint of the Rohen. It wasn't her place to seek them out, but she had more questions than could be answered without them.

"They will answer when they can," Khalia returned.

Again, the child was far more than Isla could ever understand. She wondered, not for the first time, if she was the right person to raise her. The right person to watch over her. The entire Complex watched over her, protected her. The girl might be in danger, but Isla wasn't sure if she should be scared for her or know that she was always safe, even when in danger.

"Tell me about Kalli," she asked.

"He is not what he was."

"He never is," Gray mumbled.

Khalia smiled up at him and took his hand. "He thinks he is something he is not."

"He was never that either," Gray said, smiling down at her. Isla wondered if he understood more than she did of the situation. She felt as though she was a step behind. Outside of the understanding of where they were and what was to happen next. Although she understood in her bones, by the hum of the world around her, just where she was. She had the feeling that what was to come was not the easy life she had hoped for the child before her.

# Five

---

Solon stared at the wall and the odd swirling pattern that moved across it. It was something he had seen before when he wasn't quite looking, when he was concentrating on something else. It was as though the world watched him, or at least something did. Despite his best efforts not to look now, the movement drew his eye. The silver pattern flowed over the wall. He was reminded of the figure he had seen amongst the trees of the cavern. He might just be losing his mind.

"I did not realise you had returned," his wife, Felice, announced behind him, making him jump. She wore comfortable dress and a sweet smile, which he could not return. She did not appear to notice the wall. "I expected you gone for some time, to assist your niece with her duties."

"She has enough help," he murmured. He had been in the mines, he was sure of that, and then he was here. In a single blink, less than a heartbeat. Although he thought he had heard the child call out in that moment. "Have you seen her?"

"Not yet," Felice said, giving him a quizzical look. "The newsflashes have all announced that she has returned to her place, but we are yet to see vision. I thought her perhaps shy. She is still so young."

"And yet so worldly."

"Truly? Where has she been schooled?"

He turned then and took her in. He was aware of where the child had been, as had the rest of the council, and they had been given little input into how she would be raised. They had been told—and he wasn't sure by whom now that he thought about it—that she was where she needed to be. To hear her give instructions, she certainly had been raised as his sister would have needed her raised. She was Hendra, and he wondered if genetics had much to do with it.

"Alice," Felice called out.

"Excuse me?"

"I asked after Alice. You would not talk of her before, and I assumed the child was with her on her home world. Has she returned?"

He shook his head. He didn't think Alice had anything to do with the child, but now that she'd been mentioned he didn't know why. She had disappeared, he thought, before his sister. Something odd had occurred in the last weeks or days of his sister being Hendra, and then she was gone. Although that wasn't right either. She had remained Hendra despite Alice's disappearance. Had the soldier who had become mother been involved in that in some way?

"What is it?" she asked, resting a hand on his arm. He jumped before he could stop himself. "I see," she said, her voice cold, and he cursed his lack of attention.

"It has been a trying time," he said, and it had been—he couldn't even explain how he was sitting in this room. "And I am distracted trying to understand what is to be done."

"You want the Complex for yourself," she said, her voice low and full of understanding.

"It is mine," he muttered, despite what the girl thought she was. "Did they call her Queen?" he asked the room. The wall seemed to ripple more determinedly.

"Who called her Queen?" Felice asked. "The child?"

"She is more than I thought she could be."

"But you still want to replace her."

He wondered if the woman was testing him. She knew who he was, what he was, and that this was his for the taking. He should have ruled in his sister's place, although she had been too strong for him. He had read the stories of the Hendras who had died young by war or accident. Never usurped, no matter the plots. Whatever the cause, if they had not produced an heir, the younger sibling had stepped in. Solon had waited, and she had disappeared long before the child had been born. Long before they could prove the child was Hendra. And yet when she had returned, if that was what she'd done, they had accepted her without question, without testing her true origins. But there was something else about the child... The idea of those eyes made him shiver again.

"Where is she?" Felice asked.

"On Urgway, or at least she was. She wanted to see the mines and what my sister had done in the name of protecting the people. I thought it a chance..."

"You left her there?"

"She is not unprotected, but then I'm still not sure how that happened."

"What?"

"Me being here," he said too loudly. Did she not understand what he was dealing with? Was she not listening? That was her role, after all. The reason she had been chosen. His father had hinted at that long ago. He had taken the words to heart when selecting his wife, even though his father was long gone and before his sister could involve herself in his affairs. She had seemed genuinely surprised that he had managed to marry and produce children. That had confirmed for him that he had managed to do as needed without her notice, or she truly had never intended for him to be anything more than what he was. Although, she had been instrumental in ensuring his place as chief of this little planet. It might be small, but it still gave him control of one fifth of the solar system and thus influence at her council. Not that they had been paying him the attention they should.

"You aren't making any sense," Felice murmured, and he looked from the wall to her. "What has happened to you?"

"I'm not entirely sure," he admitted.

"What do you need from me?" she asked, and yet there was something there, something holding her back. As though she was offering what she knew he wanted and yet wasn't willing to give.

He shook his head, and she sighed before turning for the door.

"Try not to pull the children from their studies," she said as she walked from the room. He nodded, although it wasn't worth the effort as she had already gone.

He turned back to the wall, which now appeared just as any other wall. He pushed himself out of the comfortable chair and pressed his palm to the surface. It felt as any other wall should. "What do you want from me?" he asked, and the wall pulsed and shimmered as the strange pattern worked its way beneath his hand. He wanted to pull away but couldn't.

And then it was pulling at him, his hand appearing to disappear into the wall. Panic closed around his throat as though someone were squeezing him. He pulled back, but the hold was strong. Did the Rohendra want to talk to him? Did they think they could find what they hadn't with his sister, and would that be a possibility to rule in her place?

The pulling suddenly stopped, Solon's hand wrenched back with the force he had been applying, and then he staggered back and into the chair.

"Father?" a voice behind him asked. He turned slowly to take in his eldest son, Ayers. "I am sorry to disturb you."

"You don't disturb me," Solon said, motioning the boy into the room. "Your mother said you were studying."

"We are always studying," he murmured, looking down. "I want to ask after my cousin, and it has been so long since I've seen you." There was a longing in the boy Solon didn't remember from the last time he'd returned.

"She is young, but strong," Solon replied. He stood from the chair and walked around to stand before the boy, who appeared younger than he remembered and yet taller. "What have you been learning?"

Ayers shrugged as though he hadn't been paying attention, and Solon bit his lip so as not to chastise the boy. There was much he needed to know, much he needed to learn to be able to follow Solon.

"What of your cousin do you wish to learn?"

Ayers opened his mouth and then closed it.

"There was something that made you come and ask," Solon prompted.

"There is a rumour that she might not be who she claims to be."

"She is six. Could it be that there are others making the claim on her behalf?"

"Do you doubt her origins?" Ayers asked quickly.

Solon shook his head. Despite the desperate need within him to make such a claim, he couldn't. The child was so clearly his sister's child.

"Is she like my sister?" the boy asked.

Solon nodded slowly as he murmured, "No."

Ayers laughed. Solon indicated the chair, and they sat as men would to discuss the world. He realised then that he should have taken more time with the boy—not just ensuring he was learning all he should but spending the time to teach him himself. "She is a little girl, and she reminds me of your sister in many ways... and yet when she speaks..."

The boy moved closer to the edge of his seat as though waiting for more.

"She is something else entirely, and I'm not sure she learnt that from those who raised her."

"Alice," the boy responded.

"Not Alice," Solon said softly. "Although that is the assumption. An old soldier, a tutor, and another girl she refers to as minister."

"An old soldier? Don't girls need mothers?"

"She is the mother," he replied, unsure whether he really agreed with the sentiment. But it was one that had been repeated, and the child—the Hendra—appeared to treat her as such.

"Island Tarle," Ayers whispered, his focus far away.

"Where did you hear that name?" Solon snapped. The boy's lip quivered ever so slightly.

"I don't know," he murmured. "I just know it."

Solon glanced at the wall, but it was as it should be. He wondered what influence the Rohen had on them all. Was it whispering to his children as well as to him? He stood then, quick enough that the child flinched. It had been whispering, giving him ideas, reassuring him, and yet there was the strangest nervousness surrounding him. What would they gain by influencing him?

These beings, the Rohen, or Rohendra. He had no idea of what his sister had been dealing with or what she had thought she could do to save the solar system from them, but it was only now that he realised how much influence they had over his life. He hadn't ever been conscious of them there, whispering, and yet he heard it now in his son's voice.

How would his behaviour help the Hendra? Or were they planning something else?

Isla sat against the tree, feeling the solidness of it, the surety of the world around her, and yet she had the feeling that she didn't understand. "Explain to me again why the Rohen allowed Solon to take you."

"He didn't," Khalia said. "They didn't." There was a hesitation to her response, as though she wasn't quite sure herself what was happening.

"The Rohen moved you?"

"Not our Rohen."

"Not our Rohen," Isla murmured, pushing up from the tree. "I don't understand how they can't be part of the one."

The child shook her head, appearing utterly lost for a moment, and blinked back tears. "It is what it is," she whispered.

"No. The Rohendra works with us—with you as their queen—for the balance of the Complex."

Khalia actually sighed and all but rolled her eyes. She didn't need Isla explaining this to her. The usually patient child appeared more childlike than she had for some time.

"But some of the Rohendra do not."

Khalia looked then as though it all made sense. "Do they want a different balance?"

"Perhaps," Isla murmured, looking for Gray amongst the trees. He had wandered with Beth to see if any of the landscape looked familiar. Isla longed for a Reader, someone else who could explain this. "How is Kalli alive?" she murmured.

"Maybe he isn't," Khalia said. "He looked alive."

"What if he didn't die? What if the Rohen moved him in that instant?" Isla mused, remembering the dust that had settled in that moment and the look of horror on the Hendra's face as he'd disappeared between them. He had been standing beside her, then between them, and then gone. It had all happened so quickly, and no matter how many times Isla had relived the memory in the years that had passed, it didn't make any more sense. He had looked more like Kalli in that last moment than he ever had.

"I don't know this place," Gray said, coming into the clearing, the warm sun above them. "The Rohen said that we were at the core of the universe where the battle had taken place, where the Readers had plucked us and decided our fates."

"What if there are others?" Isla asked, her mind still trying to understand just what Khalia had been saying. She was sure the child said more than she understood herself. Something in the Rohen gave her the understanding, but she might not have fully grasped it. She looked over the child carefully, blue eyes glowing with the wonder of whatever she was deep inside, Hendra, Queen and Rohendra all rolled into one. For the first time, Isla wondered if the child truly was who she thought she was, a product of the previous Hendra and whatever magic the Rohendra had worked.

What if she was Rohendra herself? Yet she didn't appear to be anything like the Rohen Isla had seen. There were hints of the metal around her, but it wasn't evident on the surface. What if the Rohen were working against them and she was part of that plan? Isla rubbed at her temples.

"What is it?" Gray asked. As she refocused on them standing before her, she thought she saw something hard in Khalia's eyes.

"You are lost," the girl murmured, stepping up and holding up her hands to Isla like she had when she was very little, to be picked up.

Instead of picking her up, Isla squatted down before her, and Khalia placed her hands gently to the sides of her face. "They are one, they are many," she whispered, but there was something in the way she tilted her head.

"Can you read the thought?" Isla asked, wondering if it would be easier if Khalia saw what was swirling around her mind rather than trying to find the words for it.

"It can't be," the child whispered, and as Isla looked into her bright blue eyes, there was a touch of silver there, a thread that wove itself around her soul. "It isn't possible."

"What isn't?" Gray interrupted.

"Mama thinks there is some Rohen working against the Rohendra, or differently. It is what I understood, but it is confusing," she murmured.

"Is it possible for part of a collective to work against the majority and them not know?"

"They know it all," Khalia whispered. "They are one."

"They may not be."

"No," Beth said, her voice clear and echoing through the trees. For a moment, Isla might have thought they were underground, Beth's voice echoing off the cavern walls.

"Do you mean it isn't possible or that they may, in fact, not be one?" Isla asked.

"It can't be. The Rohendra have kept the balance for so long within the Complex. They are the Complex. It couldn't be possible for another group to work within the group. Or what we fought for on Urgway and against the previous Hendra no longer matters," Gray said.

"It matters," Khalia whispered.

"Of course it does," Beth said. "They knew what was coming. They could see Khalia as the future. They would have seen if some of them were not working for the collective. I don't think it is possible."

"But something took Khalia to Kalli. Something saved Kalli. Something is protecting Solon, and he is keen to take over as Hendra." Isla couldn't not see now that there was a divide within the Rohendra, but it was one they could not see themselves.

"What might happen if that idea overtook the ideals of the collective?" Gray asked.

Khalia shook her head, but there was something of concern still present, as though she were sure of the Rohendra and not at the same time. She appeared to be a confused child.

"Balance," Beth repeated, although her eyes were closed as though she was listening to the hum of the universe around her. Isla did the same. She had felt this earlier, felt something not right beneath her fingers, but it wasn't making any sense. The Rohendra worked together and had done so to put Khalia in place. They wouldn't take her now, wouldn't risk her after all that had happened, including nearly losing a planet and the forests hidden within it.

"We ask," Isla said. "We have worked with the Rohen. Beth has her whole life, and as tutor you have a connection, as does Khalia. We ask the Rohendra," she murmured again. Khalia had said the Rohen were here, that this was the centre of it all, and she was certain this was the place to keep them safe when they asked the question.

Despite these concerns being voiced, the Rohendra were not appearing—not answering the question that was starting to eat Isla from the inside. The idea that they might not all be working towards the same goal scared her, and her fear grew as she watched the child move between the trees. Everything she did was for Khalia. Khalia had been created for the balance of the Complex. If she were in any danger from this, Isla wasn't sure how she could protect her.

That had been her role, to keep Khalia safe, watch over her as any mother would, and she loved Khalia as though she were her own. And yet the child had been pulled from her protection in a blink, without any hint as to who had taken her or why, and Isla had not been able to do anything to stop it.

Khalia had managed to return. Isla wondered then if Kalli might help them. Perhaps he would protect the child just as they had, despite being used by others. She looked to Khalia, wondering if she might be able to find him again, but the child shook her head. Despite the turmoil swirling within her, Isla smiled. Khalia would always be more than Isla could understand, more than a child.

"Why aren't they coming?" Isla asked.

"They are here," Khalia said. Although Isla could feel the Rohen in the surroundings, she needed them in a form she could talk with.

"They won't come," Beth murmured.

"Why not?" Gray asked, but Isla noted that he too was watching Khalia rather than Beth.

"They won't come," she repeated.

"Can we go to them?" Gray asked what Isla was thinking.

"Not this time," Beth whispered.

"Then we should return to Central," Isla said, unsure what they should do next. "Hendra went to Urgway and hasn't returned. There will be worry."

"The council is not there," Khalia said.

"It doesn't matter. That is where you should be."

Khalia looked around sadly, as though she didn't want to leave the trees, and reached for Isla.

# Six

---

G ray stood at the window and listened to the murmuring of the council around the table. Several of them had not been happy that he was allowed to stay, but Khalia was still a child, and it was his place to watch over her wherever she went.

Beth sat at the table with the chiefs as they spoke. Although they didn't seem to mind her, Ebberah watched her too closely, more than anyone else. Khalia sat silently at the head of the table, listening to every word. Despite his knowing she was far more than they thought, she appeared to be a child today. When she yawned, moving quickly to cover her mouth, he stepped forward.

Isla was sitting at the desk. She looked up from her reading but didn't say anything. For a moment, Gray was frustrated that the small child he had watched grow should be subjected to sitting for hours through these long meetings. As he approached the table, Khalia held up her hand as though to indicate he stop. He raised his eyebrows and turned back to Isla to see what she thought, but she was focused on something else, something far away. She hadn't quite been herself in the short time since they had returned from Urgway.

Isla was so sure that things were not as they should be. It had been strange that Solon could take Khalia, and yet she had returned on her own. He wondered if there might have been some mistake. It wasn't possible, as Beth was so sure, for any of the Rohen to work against them.

Khalia turned and took Gray in as though reading him, and he knew the child was far more than what she appeared. She was far more then he fully understood. "There is something I need you to do," she said, standing on the chair and motioning him forward. A murmur rippled through the council.

They had been slowly explaining all that had occurred since her birth, or at least the disappearance of the previous Hendra and how they had managed the Complex. Gray doubted they were sharing everything they had done, and that they hadn't maintained some control for themselves.

Khalia wrapped her arms around his neck and pressed her cheek to his. She sighed and leaned her little frame into him, and he wrapped his arms around her to keep her steady. "Go to Alice's room," she breathed, her voice barely audible.

He waited, sure some other instruction was to follow, but she only kissed his cheek and released her hold. He stepped back as she sat down, the room silent.

"Go on, Chief X'ang," she said, her voice sweet although it sounded as tired as she appeared to be.

Gray waited. With no further instructions and Isla apparently lost in thought at the desk, he turned and headed out through the private lounge as Hendra had instructed him to do. He ran his fingers over the walls as he walked, thinking of the dark corridors hidden behind the world those who usually walked these hallways knew. A breeze touched his fingertips. He pressed his hand to the wall, and a door opened.

As he stepped into the dark, he wondered if anyone could find it or if the door only opened for a few. But these had been Calder's tunnels, and he was long gone even if Kalli appeared to be alive somewhere. Gray had no idea where, nor did Khalia. Somewhere in the trees. It was odd the man would hide so close to the Rohen, and yet it made perfect sense. If the Rohen had brought him back from the dead, he might not be hiding at all.

Gray walked through the dark hallway, his fingers still trailing along the walls, and then in the distance he saw a pale light. A touch of green tinged the square of light that marked the hallway. He raced forward and into the room that had been Alice's. Gray still didn't know whether Alice had been aware it wasn't a secret or truly thought she had found a sanctuary.

The door closed behind him with a quiet swish and click. A light layer of dust covered every surface, as though someone still used the place but hadn't tidied in some time. He took in the small space, thinking that it had appeared so much bigger when he had been here before. He walked through to the bedroom, the dishevelled sheets dark with long dried blood. He moved through into the bathroom, which was in a similar state, cloth and torn clothing abandoned on the floor.

Had they left it like this when they had run? They had been injured—he had been quite a mess—and yet he was sure it had been cleaned up and sorted.

He walked back out to the seats that hugged the large square table in the middle of the room. He sat heavily in an armchair; it was a snug fit but reminded him of the chairs in Minister Burre's library. He ran his hand over the rough texture, remembering the fear of letting go of Isla as she leaned over him, feeding him tea. Her face had been worried and smeared with his blood.

"Why here?" he wondered aloud.

"We are always close, and yet not always close enough," a deep voice vibrated through him. He looked around the room and saw no sign of the Rohen.

"Do you fear what we might do?" Gray asked.

A soft chuckle followed.

"Do you fear the others?"

Silence fell, and Gray wondered then—if Isla was right, which faction was this? Which of the Rohendra wanted to talk with him? They must have trusted Khalia, and she would not have sent him here if the Rohen who had worked against her were in Central.

Or did she not know?

"Island may be right, but she is wrong," the voice whispered. A silver Rohen being walked from the wall and sat slowly on the couch opposite where Alice had sat so long ago—and yet it appeared as though she had only just left the room.

"You don't believe that some of the Rohen may be working for a different outcome?" he asked.

The being remained unmoving in the opposite seat.

"Explain how Kalli lives," Gray insisted.

"I cannot," the being hummed. "We cannot. He was lost to protect the mother."

Gray nodded once. Isla had blamed herself so long for his death. That she had worked to save him just for him to sacrifice himself to keep her safe. And yet in some ways it made sense to Gray. That was why they'd needed him—that was how he was to help Isla. Kalli, when they'd found him buried deep within Calder, was to save her.

"And taking Khalia from the mines?" he prompted.

The being shook his head, strangely fluid and yet jerky at the same time, as though it wasn't something it had done before. "We would not put the queen at risk."

"Maybe someone wants a new queen, a new Hendra."

"Solon is not that man."

"Not the man to be Hendra, or there is another?"

Despite the smooth, unseeing face of the Rohen, it appeared to Gray that it was peering into his very soul.

"There is no other but Khalia. There will only be Khalia."

Gray opened his mouth and then closed it. It was a strange thing to say, and yet Gray felt something in the words that scared him enough that he didn't want to ask the question. Didn't want to know what further challenges she might have to face. He knew he would be standing there beside her, or at least behind her in whatever she did, but the niggling feeling in his chest worried him.

"We will protect her."

"All of you?"

"Yes," it hummed, the sound soft, and yet the confidence behind the words flowed over Gray. He took a breath, not realising he had been holding himself so still.

The Rohen stood and moved around the room. It appeared more like a man than Gray had previously thought, and he expected it to start pacing. "Island thinks we are corrupted."

"She is worried that you may not all work to the same ends."

The creature stopped. Again, despite its featureless face, Gray felt its gaze bore into him. "It cannot be."

"So Beth said."

"And yet there is worry; there is something Hendra fears."

"Khalia is worried?" Gray asked, standing and looking towards the door.

"We will protect her," it repeated, although there was something not quite as confident in the feeling that washed over Gray or hummed through him. Before he could ask anything further, the Rohen was gone.

Gray stood in the doorway to the office and watched the quiet conversation continue at the table. Isla still sat at the desk, but she had slipped forward, her head resting on her arms. She was likely asleep. He worried that she'd been working over the same thoughts and it was taking its toll.

He looked from her to Khalia to see the child watching him.

"I think it time to retire," Ebberah said. Gray was surprised not that she mentioned it, but that everyone around the table nodded in agreement.

Khalia had sat back in her chair, her legs crossed as though she sat on the ground. She too nodded.

"Thank you," she said. "I understand more of what you have done, and why," she added, looking more at Chief X'ang of Urgway. He bowed low. "I only want for balance," she said.

They waited around the table, all standing, and when Khalia unfolded her legs and stood on the chair, Gray stepped forward. "Tomorrow," she said softly as she leant into him, her arms wrapping around his neck. He pulled her close, and she rested her head on his shoulder. He stood watching the chiefs file from the room. Ebberah, the last to leave, turned and looked back at them.

"Is there something else?" Khalia asked without looking up.

"You will keep her safe," she murmured. Gray wasn't sure if it was a question or statement.

Khalia lifted her head to the woman at the door. "Why would you doubt?"

She shook her head, hand on the door, but she didn't move.

"What worries you?" Gray asked. "Tevia helped us in the past."

Ebberah pushed the door closed after the others and folded her hands in front of her. Gray glanced over his shoulder at Isla still sleeping at the desk.

"I have seen little of her since that time," Ebberah said.

"She has a closer affinity to the Rohen than her family," Khalia said. "You could not have kept her."

Ebberah opened her mouth and then closed it.

"I have not seen her," Khalia added.

Ebberah looked down at the ground.

"Do you fear her involvement with them?" Gray asked.

She shook her head, but he sensed something else—a hesitation perhaps, uncertainty.

"I'm not sure what it is," she said, stepping forward. "I cannot name it, but there is something that scares me."

"The Rohendra work for the Complex," Khalia yawned.

"That is not what concerns me. I understand there is more to the world than I could ever fully be aware of. That the Complex is more than I understood it to be. It is the child herself who scares me."

"Tevia would no longer be a child," Gray said.

"She will always be, and there is much still that is very childlike. I should have sent her away. I should have tried to help her in other ways."

"She would not have stayed with us," Beth said, drawing Gray's attention and reminding him that she was sitting at the table.

"Do you know her?" Gray asked, then shook his head. Beth understood the Complex on a different level. She knew of everyone within it because the Rohen did. He wasn't sure how they shared with her their information.

"She did as she was required, as she was led to do. She works within the Rohen. She always has," Beth continued as though he hadn't asked the question.

"I understand that," Ebberah said.

"And so why does that worry you?" Gray asked.

"I cannot explain it, but it does."

"Could she be...?" Gray didn't know how to phrase the thought forming in his head. He had only just conversed with the Rohendra claiming that they were one. Yet there was the chance that the child who had helped him all those years ago, who had led him to the minister and Beth and the other children, was working for something they couldn't understand.

# Seven

---

I sla dreamt of strange shapes amongst the trees that hid from her, and yet she could see them clearly. They both were familiar and unknown, and she didn't know if they were friend or foe. She woke with a start, her neck stiff and the office dim. The table that had seemed so full of conversation during the day was empty, as was the room around her. She wondered at Gray leaving her alone, but he might have been more focused on Khalia. The idea made her smile.

She wasn't sure at what point she had laid her head down on her arms, when she had tried to think over the strange idea of the Rohen and listen to the conversation around the table. It seemed that so much had occurred while they were at the colony, most of which she wasn't really aware of. But then, her role had been to raise a child, and the council appeared willing to share the history of the Complex since the Hendra had disappeared.

It was still hard to consider Khalia as Hendra, and yet she couldn't be anything else. She was everything Isla had thought she would be, and she was still a little girl. Isla's earlier fears of the child disappearing had vanished when she'd settled in at the table with her council. She was so in control. If the Rohen or Solon or anyone could take her away, she would be the one to choose when she returned.

Solon had been quiet during the day. Responding when he was required to, giving information when requested—and yet he looked about him as though he thought there was something else in the room with them. Isla doubted he could sense the hum of the universe, the Rohen. She wondered what he thought had really occurred with his sister and what he might be willing to do if he found out the truth. Not that Isla really understood in the end what had happened to Hendra. She had been left with the Rohen, and they had delivered Khalia when it was time. What happened to Hendra after the birth of the child, she didn't want to guess. Hendra had had strange ideas. There was something she had thought her father had said that led her to believe the Rohendra were not working for the good of the Complex—or was it the good of the Hendra?

Isla pushed up from the desk and stretched her arms above her head, tilting her neck one way as far as it would go and then the other. She rolled her shoulders as she headed for the window. The city below was almost as bright as it was during the day with the lights, the vehicles and ships, the newsflashes.

What if there had been some truth to the Hendra's crazy thoughts? What if her father had discovered something similar, that not all the Rohen worked as one? Isla struggled to remember her exact words, the phrase she had used that had pushed her to try to destroy the Rohen and nearly the whole Complex.

Isla rested her head against the cool glass. The words escaped her. She wondered if a Reader, or even Beth, might be able to pull the memory from her mind. Or had she twisted them, misheard something, and her whole determination was based on nothing? Isla had believed that before, that Hendra was mistaken, simply wrong in her understanding of the Rohen. Only now her daughter was at risk, and the Rohen might not be the ones who could save her.

Isla longed for the trees, for the comfort of the bark against her cheek, the solidity of it, the calm of familiar noises and the hum beneath her fingers. The city that buzzed beneath her was familiar, one she knew well, one she had been comfortable in, and yet there were too many ghosts, too many people she didn't know or understand. Even high above it, in the silence, protected from the noise by the thick glass, she felt surrounded by danger.

She was reminded of the time she had lived in fear, the years she had slept with a duster, when she had thought the Rohen had tried to kill her. The memory was palpable, a bitter taste at the back of her throat.

"You are wrong," a voice whispered across her skin. She flinched, despite the hum that flowed with it and the familiar timbre.

"Am I?" Isla focused on the city beyond the glass, and yet her eyes found the reflection of the Reader hovering behind her. "Can you know it all?" she asked.

"We do," he hummed, his face covered by the dark hood of the cloak. She had seen them; all of them, she was sure, shared the same aged, friendly face and unseeing—or was it all-seeing—solid silver eyes.

She studied the dark depths beneath the hood, wondering whether she would know the difference if another came in his place.

"Why do you doubt?"

"I have seen it. I have felt it. She was pulled from my hold."

"Not by us."

"If not, then you would understand who would have had such skill to move the Hendra through the Rohen without her consent." She didn't want to sound harsh, but the words carried the fear she had felt when the child was pulled away. "Solon did not do that."

"Are you certain it was not the child? She may have sensed something and investigated."

"She would have said."

"Would she?" he asked, the hum of his voice making the hairs on the back of her neck stand to attention.

Isla had no doubt in the child. In *her* child. Khalia would not lie to her—she had no reason. If she decided the end of the Complex were required, Isla would follow without question.

"I see that you would," he hummed.

"You believe in her," Isla whispered.

"She is our queen. We put her here. We raised her up."

"From what?" Isla asked, a strange feeling chilling her bones once again. The world wasn't quite as she had believed it to be. She wondered if Khalia knew more in those wise words and ideas than a child of six. Perhaps it wasn't just her connection to the Rohendra; perhaps she was older than Isla had considered. Older than Isla understood her to be.

"The Rohendra is the Complex," the Reader whispered, leaning forward. "We are as old as the universe itself."

"Does that mean the Hendra could have lived before, or lives in a different form?" The idea of Alice feeding the Hendra Rohen while she was carrying the child took on a different meaning, a different idea. It made Isla shiver.

"She is as she is," he whispered.

"You didn't answer the question," Isla murmured, but there was no response, and she turned from the window to find she was alone in the office. It felt even more empty than it had when she had woken and found herself alone. Did she not understand the Rohendra or the Complex at all? Her conversation with the Reader hadn't made anything clearer.

She headed out to the lounge and through the empty building, and for a moment she wondered if she were dreaming. The duster formed easily in her hand, giving her a confidence she hadn't realised she needed, not for some time. She was reminded of the fear she'd felt when she first woke.

She breathed slowly and ran her fingers along the wall as she made her way towards the Hendra's apartment, their apartment. She missed the colony even more. She moved through the dimly lit room towards the oversized bedroom. In some ways, the oversized bed was the only place she had felt truly at home in the whole building.

Khalia was spread across more than half of it, her arms and legs out like a star. She usually slept curled either against one of them or between them, and when she slept in her own bed she was curled then too. It seemed odd, as though suddenly Isla didn't know the child. Gray lay in his usual position, his eyes closed, his breathing slow.

Isla sat slowly on the edge of the bed, resting the duster in her lap as she watched the two people she was closest to, and felt further away. Her hand closed tighter around the duster as she tried to level her breathing. She was in control; she had been in control for a very long time, and now she wasn't. She wasn't sure why.

Khalia flinched and jolted in her sleep as though something had frightened her. Her wide blue eyes focused on Isla. Within a heartbeat she was in Isla's lap, bundled in a tight ball, the duster gone and Isla's arms closed around her. The child started to sob, and Isla ran a hand over her hair. "Shh," she whispered, holding her tighter.

"I had a terrible dream," she whimpered.

"You looked... different," Isla said.

Khalia's little face peered up at her. "Did I?"

"Like a star," Isla said, nodding slowly.

"A star," Khalia whispered. "I wasn't dreaming of stars."

"Can you tell me what you were dreaming of?" Isla asked.

Khalia buried her face in Isla's chest again and shook her head vigorously.

"Ok," Isla whispered. Did the Reader know more than he had told her? Maybe she had dreamed of a life already lived. "Let's try again," she said, standing and carrying Khalia towards her bed.

"No," the child said quickly, her hold on Isla tight. "I want to stay with you."

Isla turned and headed back to the large bed. She wanted a shower, to change into something more comfortable and press herself against Gray, but she lowered the child instead, allowed her to snuggle against Gray and then sat down and unlaced her boots. She pulled her legs into the bed and snuggled beneath the blankets, the warm child between them.

# Eight

The next morning, Khalia didn't look herself. She was weary, her eyes sunken as though she hadn't slept at all. Although she had been still during the night, Isla couldn't say whether she had slept.

"Is she ill?" Gray asked as they watched her at the table with the chiefs. The conversation was slow, and she didn't appear to be paying attention to it.

"Go away," she snapped, and Isla took a step forward.

"Excuse me?" Ebberah said, her indignation evident.

"I said you can all go away. I have had enough. You are not helping me learn. You can return to your planets, and we'll meet again when I think it is needed."

"When you think it is needed?" Chief X'ang asked, standing from the table. "Not when the people might think it needed?"

"Did they dictate the frequency of previous meetings?" she asked.

Something was not right. Isla took another step forward, wondering if her fear of corruption in the Rohen could have infected Khalia—if her being dragged away by she wasn't sure what had done more harm than she had imagined.

The child looked at her as though she could read her thoughts. Isla tried not to look as worried as she felt and steady her breathing.

"Make them go," Khalia demanded like a spoilt child, and Isla stared openly. Never in her life had Khalia talked of anyone, or to anyone, in such a way. "Make them!" she shouted, standing up.

"Enough!" Gray growled, the noise making the child's lip quiver and Isla's heart thump.

Khalia looked down at the ground. The council glanced around at each other, then bowed towards the petulant child and turned for the door. Isla could hear the buzz of conversation as soon as the door closed. She wanted to comfort the little one, and yet she wasn't sure what comfort she would be.

It was Gray who stepped forward and scooped her up to stand on the chair. He took her by the shoulders and stared into her face. "Explain yourself," he said, that same deep, firm voice that made Isla pay attention.

"I don't have to explain anything to you," she said. The firm, confident Hendra.

"Yes, you do," he replied.

Her little lip quivered again as though she might cry. Isla stepped forward and then stopped as Gray held up a hand.

Khalia tried to wiggle from his hold, but he wasn't letting go. She huffed and crossed her arms.

"Khalia," he said, but his voice was a little softer. Isla breathed out slowly.

"They don't care," Khalia whispered.

"About what?"

"The Complex."

"They do. It is the reason they are here. It is the reason they watched over the solar system while they waited for you to return."

"I know that," she said, her arms still crossed, her pale face highlighting the dark circles around her eyes. "But it isn't the same."

"No one cares like you do," he said.

"No," she said, "they don't."

"But they care."

She looked away then, as though she didn't want to admit it.

"You have been so patient," Isla said, stepping forward. "What changed?"

"Nothing," she huffed, still looking away.

"Something did. You have been patient for days. Has it just gone on too long?"

"No," she said. "I just know them for what they are."

"And what is that?" Isla asked as Gray opened his mouth and then closed it.

"Men," she growled, her voice low and not her own.

Isla had the same odd sensation that the hum of the universe wasn't quite right, wasn't as it should be. She wondered at what point the Rohendra would sense it. Her fear of the corruption of the child resurfaced with a vengeance. "They are the same as you are," Isla said.

"No one is the same as me," she replied quickly, but she sounded sad about it, as though she didn't quite fit.

"Do you miss the colony?" Isla asked, wondering if the other children could help her. They were all older, and yet they had all grown together.

She shook her head, and Isla was disappointed that they couldn't return to the trees she was sure would help them both. Khalia still held the same pose, but there was something sad in her face, and her shoulders had sagged.

"Tell me of the dream," Isla said.

Khalia looked up then, fear in her blue eyes as they met Isla's. She shook her head.

"Something has scared you. If it was only in a dream, it can't reach you."

Gray looked at Isla, his brow creasing.

Isla didn't understand enough of what the child was. The longer they were here, the less she seemed to know, and it scared her. If she couldn't understand what the girl was other than her own, then she wouldn't be able to understand when she wasn't herself. Maybe she wasn't corrupted as Isla feared; perhaps this was what she was, what she would become.

Gray rested a hand on Isla's shoulder. She gave him a small smile, thankful to be pulled from her thoughts.

"What if it has already happened?" Khalia asked.

"Then it cannot be something to be feared," Gray said.

"I don't think you understand," she whispered, unfolding her little arms, something of the confident child returning.

"Then explain it to me," he returned, his voice soft and coaxing.

She shook her head, looked back at the table and then climbed down from the chair. "There is something I would like to see," she said.

"Then we go together."

She led the way from the office, through the lounge and along hallways Isla was sure she had never seen before, levels of Central she hadn't realised existed. They walked and walked, but at no point did Khalia indicate she had found what she sought.

Solon stood in the room he had been allocated at Central, the suite of rooms and where he had spent most of his life before he'd gone away to school and then returned to before he'd been gifted his own planet. But it had never really been his. Hendra had ruled it all. She had reminded him of that often enough, and now he could see her in the child who had thrown them out of the meeting.

He had been surprised with how in control she had been before she wasn't. It was odd, but he feared for the child in a way, as though she might not be what they hoped. No, that wasn't it. He actually feared for her safety. Perhaps she was ill. He remembered his sister's illness, when they weren't sure if she was poisoned or sick, and the odd scans that the doctors had tried to read.

He moved back towards her office, wondering how he could suggest such a thing. But as he reached the door, the narrow-pointed silver star of the solar system seemed to move. He blinked, wondering if the secretaries who faced each other on either side could also see it.

"She has gone out," one of them said. "Would you care to leave a message, Chief?"

He shook his head, his fingers reaching for the door. But they stopped just inches away, and he wondered at the metal that surrounded them. They did not have the control they thought they had. His sister was right, and yet he was sure she had been very wrong.

Solon shook his head, the strange sensation buzzing through him. He turned back for his rooms. On leaving the office, the council had agreed that it would be better to wait rather than head back to their respective planets. There was much to do with the new Hendra, and if she was going to be fickle in sending them away, she might call them back just as quickly.

Tempted to visit with Ebberah, Solon detoured towards her rooms. But before he was even halfway there, he changed his mind. She was not acting as herself either. She watched too closely, too longingly. As though there were something in the Hendra she wanted. She had tried to lead an uprising previously and, when his sister had first disappeared, he had thought Ebberah and Oric involved. And yet they hadn't been. Oric had suffered as much damage as the rest of the planets, although no one had suffered as Urgway had. The cavern and the Rohen and the healing of the planet came to mind.

Shaking his head, he headed back into his own rooms and then stopped, fearing he had wandered mindlessly into another suite. But a look around confirmed it as his own space. A man stood staring at the wall, his back to the door, hands behind his back. His longer blond hair appeared to move on its own.

"Can I help you?" Solon asked.

"I thought I might be able to help you," the man returned. As he turned, Solon stepped back, almost tripping over his feet. "Hello, Chief."

"You are gone."

"No, I'm here," Colonel Calder said, although there was something very different about him. "I go by Kalli now."

"Kalli?" Solon asked. "One of those who died when Island Tarle survived?"

The man raised his eyebrows. His smile, although it appeared genuine, scared Solon more than he could say. "You know more of the history than I gave you credit for. Your sister always thought you dim. She talked of you as though she had to help you through life."

Solon blinked at the candour of the man, and that his sister had given him enough thought to even consider what he was capable of. "Did she?" he asked.

The man nodded. He certainly looked like Calder, and yet he didn't at the same time. The longer hair, the casual clothing—if Solon had seen him anywhere else, he might have just assumed the man a stranger on the street.

"Why have you returned?" he asked.

"I want something," Kalli said. "And we feel you will help us get it."

"What might that be?" Solon asked, uncertainty growing in his chest.

"The queen," he replied.

"Queen," Solon repeated. Had he heard that already? Had she been referred to that way? She was Hendra first. And earlier she had been a spoilt child. In many ways, it had reinforced for him that she was indeed his sister's child. He could imagine her throwing such a tantrum, but the child had been so in control from the moment she had returned that it had unsettled the council. "Do you know what she is capable of? She can move through walls, across great distances. I think she might have moved me between Urgway and my home planet."

"She is a child of six," Kalli returned, the same relaxed smile on his lips. It was more unnerving than Solon wanted to admit.

"She is far more than what she appears to be," Solon said, then looked closely at the man. Behind him, the wall appeared to shimmer.

"I appreciate that," he said.

"Do you? And those who follow her everywhere? Can you even be sure that she is my sister's child?"

"Yes," he said, a confidence there that Solon couldn't understand although he also knew it to be true. She had been gone for so long, and yet she was so clearly the Hendra.

"What would you do with her?"

"It is not my intention to harm her," the man said. "She is the queen. Tell me of the others," he prompted.

Solon refocused on him. This was not the man he had known as Calder. Solon wondered if he was connected to the man who had died.

"The old soldier acts as though she is the child's mother," he said, surprised by the disappointment in his words. "The tutor could be her father. He certainly spoke to her as though he was. And yet, it is hard to understand their connection. They treat her as Hendra and as a child at the same time."

"What do they call her?"

"She is Hendra, what else could they..." Solon stopped. In the cavern, she had told him that she had another name. That she was something else. "Khalia."

The man sighed.

"Is this because they raised her away from Central?" Solon asked.

"It was decided long before that," the man said. "Long before her mother was Hendra."

"I don't understand," Solon murmured.

"Of course you don't. But you will, or at least you can, if you choose to."

"How can I bring her to you?"

"Go to her as a concerned uncle. And you will find a way."

Solon looked down at the ground, wondering how he could find a way to do what this man asked and if it would benefit him in the end. He clenched his fists. When he looked back, Kalli was gone and the wall no longer shimmered.

# Nine

I sla knew there was something not right with Khalia, but she wasn't sure if it was the corruption she had feared or something else. She had worked hard, listened and talked to many since they had arrived. Although that had mostly involved the council, and Isla was aware of how much work it had been.

But Khalia's behaviour had been so out of character, and the following unsettling feeling in the hum of the universe worried her.

"What would you like to do?" Gray asked, standing over the child who sat pouting on the floor of the office.

"I can't find what I know is there," Khalia murmured.

"I would like to take her back to the trees," Isla said.

Khalia looked up, but said nothing.

"We were in the trees when this"—he waved his hand as though trying to find the right word on the air—"started."

"Nothing has started," Khalia said.

"Something has," Gray said as Isla thought it. "You are not yourself. What else happened when you saw Kalli?"

"I have told you," Khalia grumbled, sounding like the child she appeared to be. "Something took me."

"Something?" Isla asked.

She nodded, more of the familiar child reappearing in her features. "Maybe it isn't Rohen."

"Then the Rohen would have sensed it take you, as it must have moved through the Rohen."

"Is there no other way?" Khalia asked.

Isla shook her head. The Rohen was the Complex, it was the only way Khalia could have been moved as she was. If something were working against the Rohen, they would have sensed it. She would have sensed it.

For the first time since learning just what the Rohen was and her connection to it, Isla felt really lost. She had understanding. She knew the Rohendra in all its forms, knew the hum as she did her own heartbeat, and yet none of it seemed to make any sense. She was tying herself in knots.

"Where is Beth?" she asked, so used to the girl listening quietly around them. She had a stronger connection to the Rohen than even Isla did.

"I don't know," Gray said, looking around the room as though Beth might be sitting in a corner somewhere. "I haven't seen her at all today."

Khalia closed her eyes, her little fingers reaching out through the pile of the rug she sat on. Isla could feel her reaching out through the Rohen. Khalia screwed up her face in concentration, her eyes still closed, and Isla sat on the floor with her.

"She's not here."

"Where is she?" Gray asked.

"She's not here," Khalia repeated, opening her eyes, clearly frustrated that they weren't understanding what she meant.

"I know she isn't here," Isla said. "Where is she?"

"Not," the child repeated, her lip quivering.

"You can't find her?" Gray asked, squatting down.

She shook her head vigorously and then closed her eyes again.

Isla looked to Gray as he chewed his lip. Something she hadn't seen him do in some time. "Where is she?" she mouthed silently.

"Not here," Khalia whispered.

"We might need Minister Burre," Isla said. "He would know."

Khalia reached out and took their hands, and they were in the minister's library. Isla expected to see him bent over his desk, but the chair was empty, as was the desk. She stepped forward and ran her fingers over the wooden surface. It had always appeared covered with papers. Now there wasn't even a pile of paper, clean or written upon. She turned back to Gray, who was looking over the shelves.

"Is something wrong with the books?"

He shook his head, but he headed out into the hallway before he answered. Khalia took Isla's hand and pulled her after him.

"Beth is not here," Isla said. There was a strange emptiness to the place where it had seemed so comfortable when she had visited before.

"No one is," Khalia said, following Gray through the building, into the classroom and then into the forest beyond. The books appeared to be the only thing that had stayed.

"Did he find something in his writing?" Isla asked, and the child pulled her to a stop.

Isla looked down as Khalia looked back towards the study. "I don't like it," she said.

"Where are they?" Gray was murmuring ahead.

Isla squeezed her hand tight around Khalia's and led her out into the trees. The world had a different feel outside the house. She ran her free hand over the rough bark and felt at home, wanting to move further into the trees. She had the idea then that perhaps they should return to the colony. As they had before. As she had wanted to nearly every day since they had arrived at Central.

Something told her they would be found there, that someone would come looking and it might be worse than when the Elite had looked for her before.

"What should we do?" Isla asked the child.

Khalia looked up expectantly as though Isla might answer the question herself, but then she shook her head and focused on the path ahead.

"No ideas?" Isla prompted.

"Do you really want me to say it?" Khalia asked. "I can't see her, can't feel her in the hum." She continued along the path, her hand tight in Isla's. "It scares me," she added in a whisper.

Isla nodded as they followed Gray, although they had lost sight of him amongst the trees.

"I can't feel her," Khalia said quietly. "Any of them. Where could they go?"

"I don't know," Isla admitted. "Think about when you were moved to Kalli. What was different?"

"Something, but nothing," Khalia said, looking ahead between the trees rather than up at Isla. "It was the Rohen, but it wasn't the Rohen that moved me. It was the Rohen that allowed me to move back to you."

"Why can't they see it?" Isla asked.

"I can't see that either," Khalia said. "I can't feel it, can't understand it. It is like it is right there in front of me, and yet I can't see it."

"That is how I felt," Isla admitted. "Like the hum is off, but for some reason the Rohen can't feel it."

"They can't. I can't and yet I can."

"What do they want?" Isla asked, unsure who *they* might be. The child before her was far more like she had been prior to her tantrum earlier in the day. "Do you know what Kalli is?"

"That is an odd thing to ask," she said, her focus and gently glowing eyes zeroed in on Isla.

"Is it?"

"He is a man. A man you know and yet one you don't. One Gray understands and yet doesn't."

"What is he if we can't understand him?"

"I am not sure that he understands himself."

"And what does he want?"

"Oh, that is easy," she said, sounding like a child—her voice singsong. "He wants me."

"Because he believes you are his child?" Isla asked, her chest tightening, a sick feeling filling her. If he were working with the Rohen, if something had protected him when the Hendra had tried to destroy him, then he might work outside the hum she understood. They might have wanted him saved for some very different reason.

"No. Or Yes."

"Khalia, which is it?" Isla asked more firmly than she had intended.

"I don't know. But I think we need to return to Central."

"To the council?"

"I just think we need to return. As calming as the trees are, there is something here, something that I can't understand, and I would rather be elsewhere."

They turned back to the house. When they reached it, Gray stood on the steps looking somewhat lost.

"I want to go back," Khalia called out. He stepped down to meet them, reaching out for her, and within a heartbeat they were back in the office at Hendra Central. Solon was standing alone in the room as though waiting for them.

Solon tried not to flinch as they appeared before him. He had known they were coming, although he couldn't say how he knew. He had been wandering, thinking about the man who had appeared in his room, the tantrum of the child earlier in the day, and then he had arrived in the office. Although no one was there, he had known they were not far away. No one had stopped him; no one had tried to delay his entry or even announce that they were not there. It was his place, after all, as council and as the brother of the former Hendra, uncle of the present one, to come and go as he wished.

The child looked at him with those glowing eyes, and he was sure then that they did glow. "Khalia," he whispered. They glowed a little brighter. He wanted desperately to take a step back, but he held his ground and tried to look as confident as he thought he was. He knew the outcome, didn't he? He just had to obtain this child for Kalli and whoever it was he worked for, and then he might just get what he had always wanted. Not that Kalli had promised him that. But he had heard the whispers.

He had heard the whispers. In that moment, he was certain that he had heard far more than he had realised at the time. All that quiet time in his study and alone on the ship travelling between planets.

"No," she returned. It took him a moment to understand what she was saying. "No," she repeated.

"What do you want?" Isla asked.

"Where is the other one?" Solon asked, looking quickly around the room.

"The minister is busy," the child answered. The confidence that had both awed him and scared him when she had first arrived at Central seemed to have returned. The tantrum-throwing child of earlier was gone.

"Where?" he asked.

Gray stepped between them, the tutor blocking the child as though Solon was a danger. "Why are you here?" he asked slowly, as though Solon hadn't understood the question the woman had asked moments ago.

"I am her uncle. I was concerned."

He looked down at the child, peering around the large man, her blue eyes focused solely on him as she reached up and took Gray's hand. There was a connection between these people he might never understand. And yet he knew what he was meant to be doing, his reason for being here. The longer he looked into the glowing blue eyes that stared up at him, the more certain he was.

"He wants to take me away," the child said.

Gray pushed her behind him, and the old soldier picked her up.

"He can't take me where I don't want to go," she said with the reasoning of a child.

Yet he was an adult with more forces on his side than she could imagine. "I wouldn't be sure," he said.

"Who is he taking you for—and to?" Isla asked.

"Kalli is involved, but he isn't in control of this. It is those who exist between worlds."

"The child is confused," Solon said. He had no real idea as to who was involved in this, and he knew he didn't understand as much as he wanted to.

"I am the queen," she announced.

He bowed his head. He had meant it in a mocking tone, and yet he understood that she was what she claimed to be. Confident in his own reason for being, he reached for her, but she was too far away. It was as though there were more than her two adoptive parents between them—there was suddenly a whole universe protecting her.

Despite the uncertainty and fear of what might be happening around them, Solon smiled. He knew he had a reason to be here. He knew that he was part of what was to come. The whispered voices that had seemed like a dream suddenly became clear.

"He understands what you are," Solon said, stepping forward.

"He is not what he was," the child replied.

"He might not even exist as he did," Isla said. Solon stopped, realising that he was making his way across the room, working his way around the tutor and the mother. Reaching for the child he wanted, needed, who would give him everything he ever wanted, without even knowing who had promised him such a thing.

"Kalli is not what Kalli was," Hendra said.

"No," Solon agreed. He wasn't sure what the man was, whether he was Calder or had been something else. He was working on a different level.

Just when he thought the child was out of reach, she reached for him. The movement surprised him as her hand darted forward and rested on his arm. A strange hum covered his skin. He thought he heard a strange scream, and then he was standing in the dark again.

# Ten

---

I sla only stopped screaming as Gray closed his arms around her. The door swung open, and a secretary and soldier appeared in the doorway.

"He took her," she whimpered.

"Or she took him," Gray added in a soft whisper, breathing against her ear for her hearing only.

The same uncertainty covered her skin as when Khalia had been taken the time before. When Isla had no idea where she had gone. This time the child had understood what her uncle had wanted, fought against it and then appeared to take him away. Isla felt the ripples in the hum, and yet it wasn't as she had thought it would be. After the last time Khalia had gone, she had been something very different. Isla's fear of the corruption flared again.

"Are you sure?"

"No," he murmured, "but I can hope."

"Is there a problem with the Hendra?" the soldier asked.

Isla wanted desperately to nod, but there was nothing this man could do. "She is resting. I'm sorry for worrying you."

"Worrying me?" the soldier muttered as he headed back out the door. "You scared the life out of me." He might have still been muttering more as he wandered out the door, ushering the secretary ahead of him, but Isla didn't catch any of it. She was a soldier, after all; but there were times it felt as though all her training had gone out the window when she had become the child's mother. A different instinct kicked in.

"Do we follow?" she asked, desperate to and yet unsure if she could actually follow Khalia through the hum of the universe. She might not find her intact. "What do they want with her?"

"I can't answer that," Gray said, squeezing her tight

"Someone must be able to. Where is the minister? Where are the children? Where are the Rohen?"

Gray held her tighter against his chest. She tried to slow her breathing, taking in the scent of him. She couldn't think like this, couldn't determine what had happened or what they could do to get Khalia back. She had spent far too long trying to think of a plan, but she didn't know what the problem was. No one else seemed to be able to sense that things weren't right. She couldn't find a way to set them right.

"He had to have help," she said, taking a breath and pushing out of Gray's hold. "Solon does not have the skill. He didn't even know about the Rohen as his sister did. He was surprised at the cavern—scared even."

Gray nodded. Taking her hand, he led her out of the office and into the lounge. He sat her down and then sat beside her. It was surprisingly comfortable. She wondered why they hadn't taken the time to sit in here before. Or maybe he had with a book while Khalia had talked with the council.

Isla shook the image away. She had remained in the office, watching over them. Not that she hadn't trusted them—she just needed to be close, and not knowing where Khalia was in the universe was killing her.

She took another deep breath. "Someone or something with an understanding of the Rohen..." Isla's words faded as she thought of the council sitting around the table. "Ebberah," she breathed as Gray shook his head.

"She wouldn't," he said.

"No, but something scared her. Something frightened her about Tevia."

"Why didn't she learn with the others?" Gray asked.

"I don't know, although Beth did. Maybe she wasn't destined to work as the other children did. Maybe they already knew she was something else."

"She helped us, both of us at different times. She took me to the minister, understood that I was to work with him."

"The Rohendra understand far more of the world than we do. They used us to save a queen they already knew was coming, one they already knew we would raise," she added, thinking of the cryptic way the minister had spoken when mentioning the child's mother long before she was born. "Too many understood far more than I did, and now they are gone and the Rohendra aren't sharing with us. Could they want her for something else? Did they put her with us for another reason?"

"What reason? Why would they have begged us to help?"

"I don't know," she said, leaning into him.

"Not enough of this is making sense," he mumbled.

"I just want her back," Isla said. "Last time she was able to bring herself back. What if she can't? What if they have done something to her?"

"She is their queen."

"Is it enough?" Isla said, standing and instantly missing the security of his arms around her. She felt odd, as though her skin prickled. There was something strange moving through the hum around her, and yet she couldn't be sure if it was different or if she just thought it was. Or if she needed it to be different to explain away what had happened to Khalia. "She is just a little girl," she said, turning back to Gray.

"She was never just a little girl. And she was never really ours."

The words hurt, although Isla knew them to be true. "Then it is our place to go after her. We were trusted to keep her safe, and we don't know that she is."

"Where do we start?"

"Solon," Isla said, reaching out to take Gray's hand as he stood to meet her, and then they were standing in the front entrance hall of a grand home. She could hear people calling out in the distance, and she was sure she heard a child.

Isla took a step forward. A child raced into view, followed by another. Neither of whom were Khalia or the missing children from Draroh. The younger one kept running; the one behind slowed to look at them and then raced on.

"We don't need to be shown around," Gray said, leaning in toward her.

"I would rather they know we are here."

Solon's wife entered the foyer, several men walking quickly after her. She appeared calm. She was pretty, but not overly so.

"My husband is not at home," she said.

"Are you certain?" Isla asked.

"Yes." There was a hesitation in her voice.

"May we see his study?" Isla asked.

"What right do you think you have in my home?" the woman asked. The two men behind her grumbled and stepped forward.

"We are the Hendra's guardians," Gray answered.

She appeared a little taken aback, looking about as though the new Hendra might be standing in her hallway with them.

"She is with her uncle," Isla said, the words sounding harsh even to her own ears.

The woman opened her mouth and then closed it just as quickly. She nodded once. She waved the men behind her away, then turned and motioned for them to follow. An older boy peered at them around the corner of the hallway, and Isla pretended not to see him. The house was more impressive than the Hendra quarters. They moved through clean open spaces decorated with singular expensive pieces of art, including paintings that took up whole walls and intricate glass vases.

The woman paused at a door, which slid open as she pressed her hand to a scanner. She motioned them into the room ahead of her, and Isla was surprised by the darkness inside. Solon's wife—Felice, Isla thought her name was—clapped, and dim lighting lit up the space. There was a large desk and several comfortable armchairs. One wall was covered in thick, pale curtains, the other three walls white and bare of any artwork.

"He has an office at Central," she said.

If he had Khalia, he wouldn't take her there.

"He uses this when he is home," she went on. "He is in here a lot when he is home."

Isla moved to the desk and ran her hands over the expensive wood. As she sat down, monitors appeared above it.

"I don't have access to anything in here," Felice said, sounding a little frustrated by the idea. "I don't know how to access anything."

Isla flipped through the documents that appeared on the monitors, but there was nothing that might indicate where he had gone or what he might do with Khalia. "He must be working for someone else," she murmured.

"All he does is for the Hendra and the Complex," Felice said, the anger clear in her voice.

"I'm not sure that is true," Isla said, pushing up from the desk. She turned to the wall. For a moment, she was sure she felt something there, something that didn't hum as it should. But as she studied it, she started to think that maybe she was imagining the world to be different than what it was. She walked to the wall and put her hand to it.

"We don't have any secrets hidden here," the wife asserted.

Isla closed her eyes and listened to the hum beneath her fingers. The silver threads moved closer, reaching for her, pulling at her, and yet they stayed beneath the surface. She longed to feel them wrap around her fingers. She missed the Rohen. After so many years, she wanted the feel of the metal against her skin, wanted to see and talk with them. And although she had recently, they weren't answering her questions and they didn't want to believe what she did. Their unwillingness to come directly to her now made her worry all the more.

Solon sat in the dark against something textured and very solid. It might have been a tree, but he wasn't sure of anything. He wasn't even sure how he had arrived here. Wherever here was. He had no idea if he had dragged the child with him or if she was the one in control. The whispering that had seemed to be constantly in his ear had stopped. Despite being unable to see his surroundings, he smiled at the relief. He hadn't even realised his life had been filled with constant whispers until he had been surrounded by total silence.

When the world had first dimmed around him, he had assumed he would appear somewhere he knew. He wasn't sure why there was no light, unless they were underground again. There had been trees where he had visited before, the last time he had been moved.

He searched the surroundings again for a hint of light—for a hint of the child and her glowing blue eyes—but there was nothing. He wasn't even sure now if her eyes glowed or if that was just in his mind. He wasn't confident in anything anymore. Not what he saw or heard, not even the textures beneath his fingers.

Something brushed against his skin. He flinched, biting down on his lip to stop himself from crying out. He wanted to ask if there was anyone else around. Or if he had been transported here and would remain in the dark forever.

The silence grew heavy around him, and all he could hear was his own heartbeat, which seemed inordinately loud in the silence surrounding him. He stood slowly, using what he leaned against to help him. Keeping his hand on it, he took a small step forward. He waved the other hand around, trying to feel for something else—another tree, a wall. When his fingers met something cool and smooth, he pulled them back quickly.

"Who is there?" he asked.

The world slowly began to lighten around him with a gentle blue glow. It appeared that the light was coming from the trees. He pulled his hand back from the odd blue bark and then focused fully on the metal creature before him.

"I have seen you before," he said.

The creature slowly shook its head. If it could smile with its featureless face, Solon was sure that it was.

"I have," he insisted, looking around more at the trees. Was this the only place like this, or were there others? Hadn't they told him something about the other forests when they were beneath the ground before? "Urgway," he said.

"This is Urgway," the creature hummed, its voice odd and yet familiar.

"What do you want from me?" Solon asked.

"You have already been told what we need from you. And you have delivered."

"Kalli," he started, but he wasn't sure if he was asking after the man or if he understood that was where the instructions came from. Just who was this man and who was he working for?

"The queen is most important."

"Khalia," he whispered. The trees glowed brighter, as though they knew the word. And he understood that they did. She was connected to this place. To these creatures. "She is Rohen."

"She is the Rohendra Complex," the creature hummed. "Although not all those who share it understand it as she does. As we do."

"You are not the same as the one I met."

"As I have said."

"No," Solon said, stepping forward. "Not that you are not the one I met—you are different from him, from them."

"We are many, but we are not always one."

"What do you want?" Solon demanded.

"What we all want. Balance."

"Balance?"

The creature bowed its head and walked towards a tree. It reached for it as though it might touch it despite not appearing to have hands or fingers, and then it was disappearing into the tree. Solon staggered back. Were they everywhere? Could they emerge and disappear from nature at any time, or was it from everything? Anything? The rippling wall in his study that he never quite saw other than when Calder—no, Kalli—stood before it.

"They will not harm you," a deep voice said behind him. He turned and took in the man he had just been thinking of.

"Where did you come from?" he asked.

"I've been here for some time. Unless you willingly work against the balance the Rohendra strive for, they will not harm you."

"And if I do?"

The man smiled. Solon gulped down the rising fear and bitter taste at the back of his throat.

"They aren't the same," he said.

Kalli barely nodded, but it was enough to confirm Solon's idea.

"Where is Khalia?" he asked, worry forming for the child. If she worked for the other Rohen, these might do her arm no matter what they claimed her to be.

"Safe," Kalli said, although Solon wasn't sure she was.

"Can you elaborate?"

"I could," he said, but he clearly wasn't willing to.

"I didn't do anything to bring her to you," Solon admitted.

"You did enough."

"Exactly what did I do?"

"What are you hoping for here?"

Solon turned his back then, looking through the glowing trees, searching for a sign of the child. Or was he searching for signs of silver between the trees? He stepped away and then turned back. "Are you sending me back?"

"Do you want to go?" Kalli asked.

He wasn't sure what he wanted. It was almost as though there was something crawling over his skin. A hum of some sort, if that was the right word for the sensation. It made him shiver. He walked up to the nearest tree, focused on the blue haze that surrounded it and pressed his hand to the bark, breathing in the smell of the forest. He wasn't sure when he had last stood in a forest. But there was something familiar about the sensation.

"Where is she?" he asked again.

"Do you want to be Hendra?"

He did, with everything he had, and yet he didn't want to see harm done to the child. When had he started to care enough about her? She might not even have been his true niece, and yet he knew she was. He sighed, leaned his head against the tree and tried to slow the thoughts tumbling about in his head.

"Isla will work it out," he said after what felt like too long. When there was no response, he turned and looked around, and Kalli had gone. A strange feeling overwhelmed him then, that he was lost and alone.

He hoped that the old soldier would work out where the child might be. They had a stronger connection than Solon could understand or share. But if the child wasn't here then she might never find him. He wondered if anyone would even miss him. Isla and Gray had been there when he had disappeared from the office. But he was away from home so often it might be an eternity before his wife even thought he was missing.

He sat back on the ground and leaned into the tree as the blue glow began to dim. Before he could wonder who to ask for help, the world around him dimmed to complete darkness.

# Eleven

---

The child sat in the corner of the room, looking down at her lap. Kalli had initially worried at her silence and lack of response, but he had left her alone, and she didn't appear too distressed or upset. There were moments when he thought she was whispering to herself or talking to something or someone. But he wasn't sure. It was intermittent, and she hadn't been able to leave. Nor was there any sign of the Rohen.

She had managed to take herself home the last time he had pulled her away from Isla, and he was sure she would do the same again. This time, he wasn't sure whether she couldn't go or was waiting to find out more. He squatted before her, trying to work her out.

"You are not what you were," she said, the words clear, her blue eyes shining. He was reminded immediately of Isla's confidence.

"What was I?" he asked. *Didn't she say something similar last time?*

"You are a changeable beast. You are a survivalist," she said.

He sat back and smiled, crossing his legs in a similar manner and resting his hands on his knees. He could be whatever he needed to be. He struggled to remember who he had been before; it was what he'd thought others had needed him to be. But it was a surprise that the child could read him so well—or had an idea of who he was—from her connection to the Rohendra.

"I am Kalli," he said as she shook her head. "They asked her to save me." He wondered if that was just so that he could die instead of her, and yet here he was.

"You are not," she said, sounding like a child.

"What do you want for the Complex?" he asked.

She leaned her head a little to the side as though trying to read him, perhaps wondering what he meant by the question. "Balance," she said.

"We also want balance," he said, but she shook her head again as though she didn't believe him. "We do."

"Balance," she repeated.

"Yes."

"Balance between the planets, between the species and between the worlds."

"So that the Complex works."

"It will not work with your idea of balance."

"Why not?" he asked, wondering again just how much she understood of the universe and the plans set out for its future.

"Because that is not balance."

"The trees would be protected."

"More than the trees are to be protected."

"Many have already been lost. Your own mother one of them," he said, his words harsher than he had intended. He wondered at the feeling of loss he had for the woman. She hadn't cared for him in the end.

"Too many more will be lost, and the trees will wither."

He shook his head.

"I've seen it," she whispered, staring him down. Her blue eyes were more intense than he realised. "And she was not my mother."

He blinked. "She must be your mother. Or you would not be the Hendra."

"I am Hendra because I am Rohendra."

"Are you part of the one or part of the many?"

She smiled then, her blue eyes shining, and Kalli realised he didn't understand as much as he thought he did.

"Why do they want you?" he asked.

"That is an odd question when you are doing as they bid. You now stop to ask why."

"I've seen what the Complex is," he said. "I understood."

"And now you don't."

"I do," he said, but he wasn't convinced. Something in the confidence of the small child before him filled him with doubt.

"You are corrupted," she whispered.

He shook his head. The words did not make sense, and yet they did.

"Mama fears I am corrupted, as though the Rohen that runs in my veins is not as it should be. Is not as it was."

"Is she right?" he asked.

"No, and yet she is."

Kalli sighed. The child was toying with him, or at least something was using the child to toy with him.

The world had been something very different since he had returned to it. And yet he had understood it from the inside of the Complex, when he had been lost. If that was what it was. He had a better understanding of the hum of the universe, although it wasn't always consistent. He couldn't always understand it as he had. He wasn't sure when the understanding had come.

Now he was exactly where he thought he was supposed to be. They wanted the child. Khalia was something very different from what he thought she was, and yet exactly as he hoped. He shook his head.

"Where do you want to take me?" she asked.

He needed the queen, but he didn't know what for. It wasn't as though he had been given instructions. It was an understanding that ran through

him, whispered over his skin like the hum of the universe that he had to
have her. He would wait until he had the same understanding as to what to
do next. Maybe the Rohen doubted that he would be able to do as he was
required.

He stood, confident in the idea that he was where he was meant to be,
doing as needed for the good of the Complex, and looked down on the
child still sitting in the same position.

"I won't run," she said, looking him directly in the eye. Again, he was
reminded of Isla's strength. She was more her child than he had allowed
himself to believe, or Isla was more Rohen than he had considered.

The general paced in the office, and Isla couldn't help but watch the
door. She wasn't sure that they wanted everyone to know the Hendra
was missing, and yet they needed to be searching the Complex for her.
Despite the worry and the ache that had settled in her chest since Khalia
had disappeared, Isla thought she would be safe. That the Rohendra would
protect her as they always had. But the Rohendra were not all as they had
been.

"She moves through the Rohen," the general murmured, more to himself than to anyone else in the room.

Gray nodded, but he wasn't paying attention. He was sitting at the
table, lost in a book. Isla had longed for him to read it aloud so she would
have an understanding of what was happening within its pages. He said he
couldn't read the future, although she knew Beth had had an idea before
things happened as to what was to come. Gray had known the word for

Khalia long before she was born. She had already been growing within the Hendra's belly then, so it wasn't as though she didn't exist.

The Rohendra themselves understood what was to come. They saw what the future was, although they wouldn't share it with Isla. Perhaps they didn't see the corruption Isla was so sure she felt and yet didn't at the same time.

"She can," Isla finally answered the general. But did she want to? Was she waiting to see what they wanted from her, or did she want to remain with them? Isla sucked in a deep breath at the idea that Khalia might not want to return. She was something more than the child she appeared to be, and yet she would always belong to Isla and Gray. Isla would watch over her until she couldn't and would never willingly leave her. "She might have lived before," she murmured, and Gray lifted his head. His blue eyes were intense as he watched her, his fingers resting on the page he had been reading. "Have you seen that?"

He shook his head and bit his lip. He had the look of a man who had seen something he wasn't sure he should share with her. That worried her. What if there was more going on than she was aware? She couldn't protect Khalia that way.

"I need to know," she said.

He nodded and waved her forward. The general stopped his pacing and moved to the table to join them. "Is there something in the book?" he asked.

"Not about where she might be, but there is something odd, something I hadn't seen before that might"—he held up a hand—"*might*," he stressed, "suggest that not all of the Rohendra work as one."

"There are different forms," the general said.

"But they are all Rohendra," Isla said. "They all feel the same, understand the same. The Readers might understand more of those standing before them, but that is shared with the others. The silver forms, the liquid Rohen, the gifted."

"Gifted?" he asked.

"Beth," Gray answered.

The general looked around the room and then back to Gray. "Where is Beth?"

"They have gone, all of them, and we don't know where."

"They have just disappeared. Who is all of them?"

"Minister Burre, Beth, the children..." Gray murmured. Isla had thought he might even list Alice amongst the lost, but they had never admitted to those outside of the minister's family or the colony that she was alive. Although Isla was sure that people had guessed or understood her not to be dead. In some ways, the Hendra's death hadn't been clearly reported, and there were those in the Complex who believed her hiding somewhere.

"The Rohendra would know where they are," the general said. "Talk to them, ask them to find her."

"I think they may have an idea as to who she is with, and where," Isla said. "It is why she is with them that worries me."

"Have you talked with the Rohen?"

She shook her head, and Gray looked back to his book. They had spoken with the Rohen, but not since Khalia had disappeared a second time. It was almost as though they didn't want to come close. Again, Isla thought they might understand more than she did.

"How can we search for her without alerting the whole Complex to the fact she is missing?" Isla asked. "She has only just returned, and the panic would be more dangerous than whatever the Rohen have planned."

"And what is that?" the general asked.

"I don't know," she said. But they needed Khalia, and that was why they had allowed her to be taken.

"They understand what is to come," Gray said, his eyes on the book.

"I'll send out Elite to see if there is any unusual activity going on," the general murmured, then scrunched up his face as he pressed a hand to the communicator at his throat.

"What is it?" Isla asked.

"Solon can't be located."

"He disappeared with her," Isla said.

"Maybe you need to bring the chiefs together and tell them what has happened. They might have an idea of what to do."

"I think we might have to wait it out," Gray said, his eyes on the pages before him. "But you are right—we need to let them know."

"Do we call them in now or wait until tomorrow?" the general asked.

"I can't wait a night to know where she is," Isla said, and Gray gave her a sad look.

The chiefs looked somewhat nervous to be called back to the office, and with the Hendra not present, they seemed even more so. They sat down as indicated by Gray, the book held firmly in his hand. Isla still wondered what he might have learnt there, for he wasn't telling her everything.

Ebberah waited by the door. When Isla motioned her in, she shook her head.

"What have you heard?" she asked quickly, sure that Tevia would have shared more with her than Isla knew.

Ebberah shook her head again, not moving away from the door.

The whole group had stopped and were looking at her, as though there was something she knew that they didn't.

"Where is Tevia?" Gray asked.

"Who?" Chief X'ang asked. "Where is Chief Solon?"

"We need to talk to you about that," Isla said.

"And the Hendra?" Chief Sem asked.

"And the rest?" Chief Brown murmured.

"Who else is there?" Chief Sem asked.

Isla sighed and reached for Ebberah, who shrank away from her.

"We are not responsible for this," she said.

"Do you know who is?"

"I have an idea, but it doesn't make much sense."

"Do you want to fill the rest of us in?" Chief X'ang growled.

"Ebberah, please." Isla indicated the table again. Ebberah stepped forward, although she wouldn't allow Isla to touch her, and when she reached the table, she stood behind her chair rather than sit. "Can you tell me about Tevia?"

"She is gone," she said, looking at Gray rather than Isla. Isla wondered if Ebberah might think he knew where the girl was.

"You need to explain what is going on," Chief X'ang demanded. "Or do you think that you are more in control here than the Hendra? She might be a child, but we know what she is."

"Do you?" Chief Brown asked.

Chief X'ang gave him an odd look and then looked back to Isla.

"The Hendra is missing," Isla admitted, and there was murmuring in the group. "Her uncle has taken her with either the help of the Rohendra or for them."

"The Rohen has taken her?" Brown asked.

"The minister and the children are also missing," Gray added. "Something isn't as it should be."

"Much isn't, if the Hendra is missing and we aren't turning the Complex over to find her." X'ang leant back in the chair and crossed his arms.

"The Elite are looking," the general said, appearing in the doorway. Isla tried not to sigh. He wouldn't have interrupted a council meeting of the previous Hendra. Although the previous Hendra likely hadn't entertained them in her office. They had moved in when the she had disappeared and were here still.

"She is a child," Ebberah murmured.

"We are well aware of what she is," the general returned.

Isla wondered then how wrong they might be. That the child she thought she knew was something else. She looked at Ebberah standing by the table and understood her much better than she had previously. What she wouldn't do to keep her daughter safe.

"But not where she is," X'ang said. "How could Solon just take her?"

"It is corrupted," Ebberah murmured.

Isla studied her as she stared unseeing at the table. There was more to Tevia then. Isla wondered which side she had been working for all this time. Did she know what was to come?

"We can trust Tevia," Gray said.

"No," Ebberah said.

"What has happened?" Isla pressed.

"She..." She shook her head, unable to finish as her voice caught in her throat.

"You are not explaining anything. Are we to continue without the Hendra as we did before? Or do you think we can find her better than the soldiers who should have been watching over her in the first place?" Chief Sem asked.

"We could not have prevented this," the general insisted.

"Why not? She is a little girl. And her uncle is well known around the Complex. Wherever he is, he could be easily found."

"We can't trace him," Isla said.

"Are you saying he might be in as much danger as the Hendra?" Sem asked, and Isla wondered then just what Solon's role in this might be. He had likely done as directed in the hope for more power, and yet whoever he thought was going to give him that would likely not share any power with him. Or anyone else. She looked to Gray then as the thought took hold. What if the Rohendra didn't want to share the Complex anymore? What if their plans for balance tipped the scales?

"Mother?" someone asked. Isla blinked back to the room, looking round the group and then at Chief Brown, who had climbed to his feet.

"Did you call me Mother?"

"That is your title," he said, and she bowed her head. She wasn't sure what she was without Khalia. And now she didn't know if she was working to find the child or the child was working against them with the Rohendra. But then, she didn't know if the Rohendra were all working against them. Chief Brown knew what they were, or at least the connection to them.

She opened her mouth to ask, and Ebberah squealed. X'ang swore loudly as Isla blinked at the group.

She turned slowly to find a Reader standing behind her, tall and lean, hidden in the depths of the rough, black cloak.

"You are wrong," his deep voice hummed through the room.

"Am I?" she asked.

"Yes. We are the Complex."

"What are you?" Sem asked, his voice shaky.

The tall creature sighed. The sound moved through the room like a wave, and Isla could feel the disappointment in it. Not that they didn't know what he was, but that he was having to tell them.

"Where is Tevia?" Ebberah demanded.

His head tilted a little to the side as though reading her, but he did not respond.

"And the minister and his children?" Brown added, his voice more secure. "Is the Rohendra doing this?" he asked.

"We can't feel them. Khalia can't feel them in the Complex," Isla murmured.

The Reader looked at her as he raised his hands and lowered the hood to reveal a concerned face, his silver eyes focused only on her.

"Mother," he said slowly, "that is not possible."

"Can you sense them? Can you tell us where they are?" Gray asked, coming to stand behind her.

The silver eyes didn't appear to move from Isla.

"The hum of the Complex is off," she whispered. It was the only way she could explain it.

"She is the Complex," the Reader hummed.

"So where is she?" Isla demanded, and then he too was gone.

# Twelve

---

Khalia watched the man walk slowly across the room and sit down in a chair. He didn't move naturally. She wanted so much for the feel of the forest beneath her fingers, or her mother's warm hold. But this was something she had to do on her own.

She had heard of his death, understood the impact of it on her mother, and yet he didn't quite appear to be here. He had changed—she had felt that early on and reported the same—and yet it was more than that. He wasn't what she had thought he was. She knew the Rohen, the flow of metal all around her—she was Rohendra and yet not. She was linked to them and knew how important she was, and how insignificant in the face of the whole universe.

She would ensure balance. That was her place, after all, the whole reason for her existence. The man before her studied her from across the room. His friendly face didn't cause her any fear. Yet the odd hum that surrounded him made her nervous. She had felt something similar around her uncle, understood that he was not as he should be. Yet she couldn't quite name what that was.

A young woman appeared across the room. Kalli hadn't noticed her yet, but the feel of her rippled around the room. She was lost in the wall, and for half a heartbeat Khalia thought it was Beth. She closed her eyes and tried to picture Beth's usually serious demeanour, which would disappear the moment she smiled at Khalia. There was a connection between her and Gray. Not like his connection to Isla—that was something very different, forged long before either of them had appeared in the world.

She breathed out slowly as she opened her eyes. The woman had stepped out into the room. She was there, solid and dirty, and yet not in the same instant. Khalia blinked to be sure she wasn't a figment of her imagination.

The hum in the room had changed. The odd feeling Mama had mentioned made sense despite it being contained. As though it didn't move through the universe as it should, as though it were shielded or separate from the true hum of the Complex.

"That is why they do not understand," she whispered, pushing herself to her feet. She stumbled as her legs were numb. How long had she been sitting in that corner? "That is why they don't believe her."

"Who don't they believe?" Kalli asked, not looking at the woman. Khalia wondered if he could see her or understood that she was even there. Perhaps neither of them were.

Khalia blinked several times. She wanted to understand, wanted to know why the hum was not as it should be and why the Rohen was doing this, but she wanted to return to Gray and Mama. They were key to the balance. They had been before. And it might be that they were the only ones who understood things were slipping out of balance now.

"You cannot do that from here," the woman said, sounding like a child.

"Tevia," Khalia said.

She bowed her head.

"You work for the balance; you delivered Gray to the minister. What is this?"

"It is what is needed for the balance of the Complex. We have worked hard for so long, and the Hendra fought against us."

"She didn't understand," Khalia said. But she wondered then if perhaps she did. Was it possible her grandfather's words had not been confused, that he in his time had sensed or understood that not all the Rohen worked together? That not all the Rohen wanted the same form of balance?

"You have seen it," Tevia said. "You were there."

"Where?" Khalia asked. She had lived her whole life in the forest of Rennet before moving to Central. She had visited other places, sensed the network of the hum of the Complex, knew the Rohendra as though she were a Reader, but she didn't understand any of this.

"Before." Tevia looked at the man in the chair who watched Khalia too closely, as though she were more to him than he had said, and who still didn't appear to acknowledge the woman standing in the room.

"Before what?" she asked, frustrated at not understanding.

"You were before."

"What?" Kalli asked.

But as Tevia had spoken the words, Khalia had understood—felt the truth in them. Not that she as a person had lived before, but the Rohendra within her was all knowing. It was connected to more than the collective; she understood all that had gone before. She sighed with the relief of the knowledge. That was why she knew what she did, understood the lies men told her. Solon.

It was the reason she had become so frustrated with them that morning, why she didn't want them there, didn't want to be part of the creatures who worked to destroy what she had tried—what *they* had tried—for so long to maintain.

She was Hendra, but she was Rohendra. She was all. Something shifted in the room. The odd feeling in the hum disappeared, and she reached out.

It all made sense and yet confused her more.

As the hum of the universe settled around her, she felt calmer, although she couldn't understand the odd feeling she'd had moments before. The woman who had stood before her had gone. Kalli stood slowly, as though he was going to approach her again, and she longed to understand what he wanted.

As she opened her mouth to ask, Mama appeared before her, large tears tracking her checks. She dropped to her knees and threw her arms around Khalia, holding her so close she wasn't sure she could breathe, and yet it was the only place in the universe she wanted to be.

"I couldn't find you," she whispered.

"Something isn't right," Khalia returned.

Mama released her reluctantly, still holding onto her arms as though she might disappear again. She leaned back, looking Khalia over as though she had said something important.

"How do we fix it?" Khalia asked.

"You are the queen," Mama said with a smile. "You will find the way."

Khalia shook her head. She wanted to, and yet she didn't understand enough to fix what no one else could see.

"They aren't all working together," Mama said.

"You were sent to bring balance," Khalia whispered.

"You were," Mama said, her voice light, as though they were sitting in a cottage tucked into the rockface in the colony—somewhere they would laugh and play and learn.

"We were safe there," Khalia said.

"I miss the forest too."

Khalia threw her arms around her mother's neck and breathed in the scent of the woman who had protected her throughout her life. The woman who also understood the hum of the Complex. She had a role to play in keeping the balance, and that was why she had been tasked with looking after the Hendra. Although it was more than that. It was more than protection—it was a mother's protection, and they had known all along that this woman would be what she needed to be to keep the queen safe.

"You sensed the darkness," Khalia whispered.

"I did," Mama whispered as she closed her arms tight around Khalia and lifted her from the floor. And for a moment, Khalia wasn't sure if they were talking about the same thing. "I can find it again," she said.

Kalli stepped forward, his arm outstretched as though to stop them, as the room disappeared and they were lost to the dark.

Isla and the child clung to each other. The fear that Isla would never find her had bubbled to the surface when she found her. All the searching of the Complex and the Rohen for an idea of her had been useless. And when she had considered that Khalia hadn't been able to do the same, the idea of searching where she couldn't see had made more sense.

There were several places that she couldn't understand as she read the hum of the Complex. Isla had started with the furthest from her, and then she was in a room with the child in her arms.

Now they were lost to the darkness, and she wasn't sure if the solid ground beneath her feet was real or imagined. They could be lost inside the Rohen itself somewhere.

"I can smell trees," Khalia whispered.

"The forest wouldn't hide from us," Isla said, wondering if that was true. But they were both connected, Khalia especially so to the Rohendra.

"I am not what I thought I was," she said.

Isla wanted desperately to see her face. She pulled back a little and saw the blue glow of the child's eyes. It was both comforting and frustrating in the same breath.

"What do you think you are?" Isla asked.

"I thought you would ask what I *was*?"

Isla's smile relaxed her whole body. Despite being lost to the darkness, this child was still everything. "Does it matter what you were? It matters what you are."

"And what am I?" Khalia asked, her voice a little shaky. Isla pulled her close again, cheek to cheek.

"Everything," Isla whispered.

"Mama, that is just to you." There was some laughter in her voice.

"Not just me. For the whole Complex."

"Can that really be?" Khalia asked, her arms closing tighter around Isla.

"Yes," Isla said, keeping her voice light. "You know what we did, what we all did to protect you, to ensure you could be what you needed to be."

"You didn't think the Hendra would have allowed me to grow to be Hendra?"

"She would've, yes," Isla said carefully, wondering how to explain that she would have tried to turn Khalia against the Rohen, or that there might not have been a Complex left for her to rule over by the time she was grown.

"I would have understood the Rohen. I always understood. I am Ro-hendra."

Isla nodded against her.

They stayed as they were for some time, and Isla too came to feel the forest around them. "What can you see?" she asked after a time.

"Nothing and yet everything."

Isla waited for her to explain, but the child didn't continue.

Isla released her tight hold on Khalia but kept her hands on her body, feeling down her arm to take her hand. As she straightened up, Isla thought she caught the silver flash of Rohen in the darkness. But the hum was different here. Off. Although she too sensed the trees, she couldn't under-stand what was around her. Or what wasn't.

"They are not here," Khalia said.

"Who?"

"The Rohendra, the missing children..." Her voice trailed away and, for a frightening heartbeat, Isla thought she was going to let go of her hand. "Solon."

"Is he missing or is he here?" Isla asked.

"Here, I think."

"Why would he be here? I thought he was working with those who took you."

"He thinks he is, but I think they used him."

Isla nodded despite the dark. She looked down at the child beside her, and all she could see in the dark was the gentle glow of blue eyes looking back at her.

"He didn't understand the Rohen when we took him deeper into the mines," Isla said.

"He didn't know that he knew them, hadn't understood the whispering and taunting over the years."

"How did they remain so hidden from the Complex?" Isla asked.

"How was the Rohen contained with the facilities they had trapped you in?" Khalia asked in return.

"You know the story," Isla returned quickly. "You know the history."

"Yet it continues. Have we learnt nothing?"

"And by *we*, you mean the Rohendra," Isla said, feeling the distance from the child again. "The people of the Complex are not responsible for this."

"No, they are not; and yet they are used to make it so."

"I don't understand."

"Yes, you do," Khalia said, squeezing her hand a little tighter.

"Do you know where we are?" Isla asked.

Khalia said nothing, and then the trees around them glowed a little. A pale blue, trying to share the Rohendra silently calling from within with the queen. Within the dim light, Isla could make out a man, but where she expected Solon, she was surprised to find Minister Burre.

# Thirteen

Gray paced the office as the tight feeling in his chest grew. There had been something like realisation or recognition flash across Isla's face, and then she had disappeared. He could only hope that she had worked out where Khalia was, but she hadn't returned. The longer she was gone, the more he worried. Where could she be? Where could they both be?

"Do you know where they are?" the general asked, Ebberah sitting silently at the table in the office.

He shook his head. He was very lost in this. "Do you?" he asked, turning to the chief of Oric. He wondered then about Tevia and what she might know, what she might be willing to share.

She barely shook her head, as though she didn't want to admit to anything.

"Where is your guard?" he asked.

"Watching over... Oric." She looked down at her hands. She was still a beautiful woman, but she was not the same confident woman she had been when Gray had first met her all those years ago. Although it hadn't really been that many years. It felt like a lifetime sometimes, and yet his years in the colony living as a small family had disappeared all too quickly.

"If she finds her, she will bring her back," the general said, as though he were certain they would be safe.

"If they can," Ebberah voiced what Gray feared.

Before Isla had disappeared, she had mumbled something about the darkness, where the world was hidden, but he hadn't understood what she meant. And then she had gone, leaving him alone in the office with the general, and Ebberah had arrived not long after.

"Tell me of Tevia," he said, his voice firm.

"I cannot," she said as her shoulders sagged. "Not because I don't want to, but because I don't know. I never really understood the child—that was clear when all of this started. She works more closely with the Rohendra than I understood. I thought she was a hummer—it was why I was willing to help you—but she is something very different."

"Who is Tevia?" the general asked, and they both looked at him.

"My daughter," Ebberah said, her tone sad. But the answer had surprised Gray, for she hadn't shared the child's existence with anyone other than Tevia's father.

"I thought the child had died," the general murmured.

"You knew she had a child?" Gray asked.

He gave a small knowing smile, and Gray realised that there was much this man understood that he might not have shared with them.

"I fear she isn't working for the Complex as she was previously," Ebberah murmured.

"You think she might be working with whatever took Khalia?"

She stared at him open-mouthed.

"The Hendra," he said with a sigh.

"How can she have two names?" Ebberah asked. "She is the Hendra. We all sensed it, all understood exactly who she was, no matter how young. Was it because you were hidden away?"

Gray shook his head. His fear had gotten the better of him, and it didn't help to chastise himself now. "The Rohendra have always known she would come."

"She is the balance."

"Yes," Gray said, slowly taking a step towards her.

"Tevia had talked of the balance, talked about what was to come, and yet I hadn't understood much of what she said. In truth, she had begun to scare me. Now she terrifies me."

"Do you know where she is?" Gray asked.

Ebberah shook her head again. "She does what she wants. She always has. But she rarely comes out of the Rohen now."

"Sorry?" the general interrupted.

"The child travels through the Rohen, similarly to how Isla does, but not," Gray explained poorly.

"She lives within it," Ebberah whispered.

"Then she must know how to reach them. There is no way Solon is able to do this on his own. Someone, a hummer, must have taken the Hendra and found a way to hide her."

"Khalia is Rohendra," Gray said. The general opened his mouth as though to say something and then closed it again. "She is the balance they sought. For her not to be able to return to us scares me."

"She may be able to but not willing," Ebberah said.

Gray shook his head. He wouldn't accept that. Khalia would return to them. She wouldn't hide from them or stay away. She understood how frightened they would be. She could have moved through the Rohen at any point—to play, to hide, to explore—and yet she hadn't.

When Beth had appeared in the colony with him, he knew that Khalia had expected her. Even though they hadn't met before, she was known to the child, despite her never leaving the valley or the forest. She understood far more of the world than either of them had expected.

"They are learning what it is, or they can't return," he murmured, trying to work out aloud what it was they needed and where they might be. Why the Rohen hadn't believed Isla.

"How can this be?" Isla asked, squatting down over the man who took too long to focus on them. "How long have you been here?"

He shook his head slowly as though it hurt to think about it, then looked around. Isla stood slowly and looked through the trees. If they hadn't sensed he was here, if Khalia hadn't sensed they were here, then she had no idea what else might be hiding behind the trees.

She looked back at the child standing beside her, staring at the man, and then she was reaching forward and putting her hand to his cheek. "Are you what I think you are?" she asked. Her voice sounded young and lost.

"It would depend," he returned with a shaky voice of his own, "on what that is."

"You are the scribe," Khalia said, and the old man gave her a smile.

"What happened?" Isla asked.

"I don't know," he admitted, looking away from them, the smile slipping. "Where are we?"

"Hidden," Khalia said.

"By you?" he asked, and Khalia shook her head. "Can you get us out?"

Khalia nodded, but she looked at Isla as though it was up to her to find a way out. Isla wasn't quite sure how she had gotten them in.

"Have you seen Beth?" Isla asked.

"Have you seen the children?"

"We couldn't sense you here," Khalia said, leaning back and studying him again. Then she leaned in and touched his face again. "I thought it was

Solon. I can't sense the hum here," she whispered, closing her eyes tight. Her hand was still on his face, and he placed his hand over hers.

"It is off," he said, looking up at Isla.

She nodded. She had felt that it wasn't right, but she still couldn't understand why the Rohendra couldn't sense it—or perhaps they could, but it was locked to them like the meteor-infused buildings and glass that prevented the Rohen from flowing through it.

"Some of them understand," she whispered, squatting down in front of the minister.

"What do they understand?" he asked, but it wasn't harsh. He spoke like a teacher trying to pull the idea from her.

"Before, when I was sent out to find the containment, I sensed it as something blocking the hum, like a black spot on my senses." He nodded, and Khalia moved around to snuggle into the older man's side. His arm slipped around her easily as they both studied Isla.

"I followed the darkness," she continued. "Where the hum wasn't right."

"You believe that the Rohendra could have done this."

"They didn't believe me," she said.

"Or they needed you to come in their stead."

"It is more than that, isn't it?"

"Perhaps," he said, coughing, and then he winced.

"How long have you been here?" she asked again as Khalia held out a cup of water to him.

He looked at it carefully as he took it, then sipped slowly and smiled. Holding the cup tightly, he lowered it to his lap.

"I don't know."

Isla didn't want to leave the child for a moment or let her out of her sight, but she took a deep breath and moved through the trees. The cavern was small. The forest brushed the ceiling and, although it looked familiar, she knew it wasn't somewhere she had been before. Or was it as the other forests were? This wasn't on Urgway; this was a little underground pocket somewhere else. She reached a wall, pressed her hand to the cool, firm dirt and sighed. Again, the hum wasn't right.

"No, I won't," Khalia's voice carried through the cavern, and Isla raced back towards her.

The light of the trees was starting to fade, and the minister was holding her tight as a silver Rohen reached for them.

"Stop!" Isla cried. The Rohen didn't even pause in its movement, reaching for the child as the minister tried to put himself between them. From this distance, Isla couldn't see anything about the Rohen that marked it as different, other than Khalia's response to it. "Stop!" she cried again, and the world went dark.

She inched forward, using the trees as a guide to make her way back towards where the minister and Khalia were. She moved silently, hoping one of them would make a sound to indicate she was moving in the right direction.

"Khalia," she called after a time, but there was no response. The world was still and silent around her, and she knew she should have stayed with them. They were struggling in this environment. Unsure of what was out there as well as what wasn't. Something in this place hid them from the world and hid what was in the space from them. She could sense the trees, partly because her hand rested against the trunk of one. The sense of connection was strong, and yet she couldn't feel the hum of the universe as she should.

"Minister?" she tried, just in case.

Silence and continued darkness were the only reply. She could have been anywhere in the universe, given the blackness surrounding her. The trees no longer glowed, as though they needed some connection to the hum to do so, to the Rohen and to Khalia who had provided that.

Now that she was gone, the connection has disappeared with it, and Isla's own connection wasn't enough for this place. She leaned her face against the tree, closed her eyes and whispered across the bark. Nothing happened. She wondered if it might be different if Gray were there with her with his Rohendra words. Would he have found a connection to the hum? She pushed away from the tree, feeling the emptiness close around her. There was more emptiness within the Complex, like it was growing or the hum was pulling back.

Khalia hadn't wanted to go—she understood there was something in the Rohen to fear. And she had never had reason to fear them before. Nor had Isla, even when she had thought they had tried to kill her. They just hadn't been as careful of her as they could have been in the middle of a fight they hadn't wanted.

Hendra, the woman determined to destroy them, the fear she had held for what they would do to the Complex, suddenly made sense. The forms her father had talked of—he had realised there was something else, something hiding in the Rohen that wasn't acting in the same way as the rest of the collective. It might be they were working for balance, but it was a very different form of balance.

# Fourteen

For the first time she could remember, Khalia felt a shiver of fear. There had been times she had felt uncomfortable, particularly since they had come to Central, but this was something very different. Something frightening in itself.

She had lost her mother again. She had moved away for only a moment to look through the trees, and they were gone. She still held tight to the minister. His arm was firm and strong around her, but she could sense the fear in him, feel his heart racing as though it were her own. His fear made hers worse.

"I do wish she would stop that," Kalli said.

Khalia opened her mouth to ask what he might mean when her mother appeared in the room. She looked as though she had been across the universe and back. She was tired, although she often looked that way of late. Worry, Khalia thought, and probably about her. But this was on a different level.

Mama dropped to her knees, huffing and trying to catch her breath.

"How far did you go?" Kalli asked with a laugh.

"I've been everywhere," she wheezed. "And I collected a few on the way," she added, looking up with a smile for Khalia despite appearing spent.

A strange sensation covered Khalia's skin, as though there was something in the hum just for her. Beth appeared, looking almost as tired as Mother, and she stumbled forward and threw her arms around the two of them. The minister hugged her tight in return without releasing Khalia, which she was thankful for.

And then children appeared, a lot of children. They also looked as though they had travelled far, but they appeared more alert than Mama.

"How?" Kalli stammered, and he flickered. Khalia leant forward as her mother took a step forward.

He flickered again, as though he wasn't quite there. And then Tevia was walking through the room, and Mother's face clouded with anger. Tevia knew the Complex, had worked for the balance, but Khalia had seen her here before.

She pressed out of the minister's hold, and Beth helped him climb to his feet. She wanted to run across the room and throw herself into her mother's embrace, but instead she waited.

"You are not doing as you should," Mama said, her focus on Tevia. Still, when Kalli flickered again, something shifted on Mama's face. "Show yourself," she called into the room. Nothing happened, other than Tevia grinning even wider.

"Your mother is looking for you," Khalia said.

"She is not my mother," Tevia returned, not turning from Isla.

Isla shook her head, but Khalia felt the truth of the words, the hum through the Complex. She was more Rohendra than human, and she wasn't afraid of that—it was what she was. Although Khalia was likely more Rohendra than any of them, she was also more human than this woman. Odd that they could both belong to something and yet in such different ways.

"You made him," Khalia said, and the young woman turned for the first time to really look at her. "He isn't." She was unsure how else she could describe the odd feeling she was getting from Kalli.

Tevia smiled then, an odd, silvery, scary smile, and Khalia wanted to step away from her. But she was Hendra, and she would not step down from anyone. She couldn't. She represented everyone across the Complex, and despite her age she understood the enormity of that, the importance of that. Until this moment, she hadn't been scared by the idea.

It was what she was—what she was born to do. She was Hendra, but she was also Khalia, Queen of the Rohendra. That was important. It was her link to both worlds. She was the link. She was the balance they had strived for, that Tevia had worked for, even against her own mother.

The part of her that was Rohendra understood that far more than the child it was contained within. That understanding existed because she had lived before. She had experienced everything that had occurred before, the stories Gray read from, the histories Beth talked of—she had known it before they'd shared it.

Tevia had said she had lived before, and the longer she stood in the room, disconnected from the Rohendra and the hum of the Complex, the more she understood it. She smiled across at her mother, who smiled in return without hesitation with none of the earlier fear she had shown.

"Who did she make?" Kalli asked. He had done as he had been required, including leading her uncle further astray. He hadn't needed much encouragement. He was what he was made to be.

"You," Mama said for her. "I didn't think you were right."

"You never trusted what I really was, no matter the name or face I carried."

Mother laughed then, the sound light. It made Khalia smile in return. It had been so long since she had heard her mother laugh. So much responsibility weighed on her that she didn't allow herself the freedom.

"You don't believe they would want to bring me back," he snapped.

"They would not have let him die in the first place if the aim were to save him," she said. "Hendra chose to end his life; the Rohendra allowed it to happen. You are not him."

"You didn't believe I was Kalli when I was Calder."

"You are neither of them," she said firmly, as though he were the child needing it to be explained.

He opened his mouth and then closed it, looking to Tevia to explain this away. But she didn't even look at him.

"The Rohendra did not allow this," the minister added.

"It was required. There are those who understand that."

"Rohen who don't think as the rest," Kalli said, shaking his head as though not understanding. Neither did Khalia. *All Rohen understands the same. All work for the same. Balance.*

"It is as it is," Tevia said. "We work towards what it should be."

"It is not balance you are working towards," Khalia said.

"It is." Tevia turned on her, something wild and silver in her eye as the man beside her flickered again.

"It cannot be balance if there is only Rohendra. They are the Complex, but not without the others."

"You don't understand what true balance is," Tevia snapped, stalking towards her. Despite the lack of Rohen in the hum around her, Khalia's mother was between them in an instant. "You are not a part of it," Tevia continued, her voice a little more subdued, but Khalia's view of the woman was blocked now by her mother's back.

"I am the balance," Khalia said, confident in who and what she was. She reached forward and took her mother's hand. Stepping up beside her, she looked up at the woman who gave her the same odd sensation as the man who stood gaping at them.

"It is not as it should be," he answered.

"No," Mama said, her voice soft as her hand squeezed Khalia's, "you are not."

"How have you hidden from the Rohendra?" Khalia asked.

"I can answer that," one of the children said, stepping forward. He smiled widely at Khalia and then bowed formally from the waist. No one had ever greeted her in such a way before. She bowed her head in acknowledgement, and he cleared his throat. "It is like the times of the containment," he said, looking more at Mama than Khalia. "She has found a way to hide within the Rohendra."

"Hide within it?" Beth asked. "It can't be possible. They are one; they are many."

"And yet, there are some who are separate." He pointed towards Kalli.

"I work with the Rohen," he said. "I was saved to help them."

"The idea of you was saved," the boy went on. Khalia searched for his name but, disconnected as she was from the Rohen, she couldn't find it. She missed it then far more than she could put into words.

She released her hold on her mother and stepped forward, reaching for Tevia, who was too quick to move out of the way. Kalli instead squatted down and waved her towards him.

"No," Tevia said.

"She is mine," Kalli said, a smile pushing at his lips.

Khalia nodded once and stepped forward. Her mother raised a hand but didn't try to stop her. "I need to understand why you would do this," she said, reaching out for him. As soon as their fingers touched, she felt the flow of the Rohen and breathed it in. Before she could consider what she might do with the connection, the boy took her hand. And then the other children followed, forming a chain. She could feel them within the hum of the Complex once more. She understood them, knew them and their connection.

Kalli was Rohen, lost to the idea of what he thought he was, what he had been led to understand. That had in part separated him from the Complex, and yet he was Rohen, would always be Rohen. Kalli sucked in a deep breath.

"You are useless," Tevia growled, and as the Complex flooded in around her, the man pulled back and flickered once more. The silver being within was clear and crisp, and then he was gone.

"Where is my uncle?" Khalia asked.

"He is of no use to you, no benefit."

"He is my uncle," Khalia said. It was all that was important—not what he was or what he had done, but who he was.

Tevia raised a shoulder, smiled the same sickly smile she had given earlier and disappeared.

Khalia sighed. She was disappointed. The other children started to talk amongst themselves of ideas, theories, and worry for others. Alice was mentioned as someone who was missing that they had not found.

The boy, Damond, continued to hold her hand.

Isla looked over the group and wanted nothing more than to sit on the floor and hold the child in her arms. The hum in the room had altered, and as far as she could understand it was Khalia who had made the change. She had reached out through Kalli, or whatever he was, to the Rohendra, and reconnected them to the Complex.

The children chattered. Although she had found most of them, there were still some missing in the gaps within the Complex where the many and the one could not see. The little boy who held so tight to Khalia stood silent, as though he too were feeling out the hum around them. She wasn't sure of his gift, but his focus was only on Khalia. Although he was a child, he was at least a couple of years older than Khalia. But as he remained beside her, holding her hand, Isla felt something else, a different connection within the hum.

The minister rested his hand on her arm, and she jumped, too focused on the children to feel or see his approach.

"Alice," she said.

He nodded. "I can't understand it, any of it. How could we be removed, hidden and then found?"

"I searched for the darkness, for the gaps hidden in the hum," Isla said.

"I understand that, but can two so easily hide from the Rohendra?"

"I fear there are more than two," she said.

"Alice has worked so closely with the Rohendra. She understands what must be done, and yet she is gone."

"She is somewhere," Isla insisted. "We just have to find where that somewhere is."

The murmuring had stopped amongst the children. Isla felt the hum shift as the Readers appeared in the room. What had appeared large and sparse when she arrived now felt cramped and overcrowded.

"Thank you," the Reader said, his voice moving through the room and across her skin. He bowed deeply towards Khalia, as the boy had done. The boy who still held her hand.

"If he was made from Rohen, then it was through the Rohen that I could reach the rest."

"He was separate." The Reader shifted uncomfortably, as though it were a foreign idea.

"How is that possible?" the minister asked.

"We do not know," he responded.

A heavy silence weighed on the room, as though the Complex itself was at risk as it had been before. Although Isla had worked with the Rohen previously to prevent the Hendra from destroying the Complex, they had already been aware that the Complex could not be destroyed. This was something new.

"He is gone," Khalia said.

The Reader bowed his head again.

"Has he disappeared?" one of the children asked. "Like she did?"

"No," Khalia answered. "What he was made from has returned to the Rohendra, one of the many."

"Tevia," Isla whispered.

"Is lost," the Reader hummed. "Although perhaps not as you would expect."

"You know where she is," Beth said, her eyes closed as though she too were searching.

"We all know where she is," the boy said. "She is no longer part of the many."

The Reader bowed his head once more, this time to the boy.

# Fifteen

---

Tevia thumped at the wall, and her fist disappeared inside it. She could sense the hard surfaces around her, but it had been a long time since she had felt them under her fingertips. She had become, or perhaps she had always been, too much Rohen. And yet she only wanted to be Rohen. Tevia resented the human part of her keeping her anchored here.

Not that she had to be anchored here. She was free to come and go through the hum of the universe to wherever she wanted, only she wasn't really sure—other than when she was directed—where she wanted to be.

She had visited most of the universe now, seen hidden forests and wonders beyond her imagination and likely those of most people. And yet she was still struggling to find a place she would call home. A part of the world that made sense to just her, where she wanted to be above any other place.

The only place she had truly felt alive was within the Rohen, lost to the hum of the universe, moving between those points where others lived. She didn't know how to make that her constant reality. She had tried to mould the Rohen, create what she needed it to be. Other than her recreation of Kalli, it had not been possible.

Then she had found others, parts of the Rohen that wanted something different. The idea was fleeting, half a heartbeat, and there were times she wasn't sure she felt or heard the thoughts. She knew beyond any doubt that they had to find a new balance, one without men getting in the way. Tevia had hoped the queen was someone keen to see balance—a universe where they could enjoy the Rohen and not worry about the men. For it was the only way.

Tevia had isolated the Rohen within her from the one and had hoped it was enough to achieve what she was so certain was necessary. But it wasn't. And now, despite the Rohen in her veins and her being lost to it still, there was something she wasn't sensing in the hum around her. It was almost as though they had cut her off. She sensed it, could travel within it and yet couldn't feel it. They no longer talked to her.

She leaned back further into the Rohen and tried to reach out to those she knew would help her, those who felt the same. But there was nothing of them either. For the first time in her life, Tevia felt alone.

She wasn't surprised when the Readers appeared before her, and she sank back further into the wall. She felt their stares, their faces unseen beneath their dark hoods. Their gaze burned her skin and pulled her from the wall.

She tried not to groan with the pain of the separation, and then a silver being, solid and tall, was standing beside her. She reached for him, but he pulled away, and she knew that even if she rushed forward the being would not let her touch him.

"You are not as we thought you to be," the Reader at the front of the group said.

She stared at the silver being beside her rather than at the Readers, their gaze still burning into her skin. She wanted to defend herself, but the words wouldn't form on her tongue. She felt the weight of her actions pushing her back, and yet she couldn't reach the Rohen. She stretched out a hand, and it slapped against the wall. She stepped back again despite the pull she felt from the Readers and hit the hard wall behind her. She could feel the hum, but she couldn't enter it. The burning sensation across her skin continued.

An emptiness opened in her chest. She dropped to her knees at the overwhelming sensation of loss and the increased burning across her skin, and then it was gone. When she looked up, so were the Rohen—all of them.

She sucked in a wobbly breath and tried to climb to her feet, but she felt off centre, unbalanced. She cried out.

Her mother rushed into the room, and she guessed she was somewhere at Hendra Central, perhaps Ebberah's rooms. Although it was unknown, it felt like a kind of sanctuary with the older woman in the room. Tevia longed for her to throw her arms around her as Island had done with the queen, only the woman who had rushed through the door had stopped, her hands gripped before her.

"What has happened?" her mother asked. Not that Tevia had thought of her in that way for a very long time, but it seemed appropriate now.

"They have gone," she murmured. For they had. There was no one whispering in her mind, no shared knowledge. The Rohen had disappeared, and her skin still burned at the idea of it.

"Who has?" her mother asked, although she sounded angry rather than upset. She should be upset. Did she not understand?

"All of them," Tevia answered.

"The Hendra? Isla?"

"The Rohen," Tevia said, shaking her head. Isla might have found them all by now. She had managed to find a few, and Khalia had managed to find a way to reach the Rohendra. Tevia should have realised she would. She had been naive to consider the queen capable of anything less. She might be a child, but the queen had been returned to the seat of the Hendra for a reason.

She sighed and leaned back against the wall.

"They have been destroyed?" her mother asked, fear in her voice.

"Who?"

"The Rohen?"

Tevia shook her head. Had the woman not been listening? Was she not aware of just what power the Rohendra had? Tevia would have done well to consider that herself.

"My link has been destroyed," she said.

"But you are a hummer," her mother replied.

"Not anymore."

The woman gaped, then turned and left. Tevia felt even more alone. How could no one understand the loss she felt? She rested her head back, thinking how odd that she had missed the hard surfaces. Now she missed the Rohen and the simple connection to everything she had through them.

Isla breathed in the hum of the universe around her as all but one of the Readers disappeared from the room. Even though his face was lost in the darkness beneath the hood, she could feel his gaze.

"Where are the others?" she asked.

"You found the children, the minister," he hummed across her skin.

"When you could not," she said, then chewed on her lip. She wanted to find them as much as the Rohen wanted them found, but she had searched the hum and couldn't find them.

"They are too well hidden," the Reader said.

"What has happened to Kalli?" she asked.

"He was never Kalli, but what he was has returned to the Rohen."

Isla nodded slowly. She had understood that the moment Khalia had touched him. She looked across at the child, who pulled from the hold of the boy beside her and raced into her arms. "How can something be hidden in the Rohen without you knowing about it?" she asked the Reader.

"I do not understand," he said, a waver in his voice Isla hadn't expected.

"She wanted the world to be only Rohen," Khalia whispered.

"And now there is no Rohen."

Khalia released her hold. Isla's arms felt empty as the child turned and reached for the Reader's hand. He bent towards her and allowed her to take it.

"Oh," she breathed, her eyes closed, and Isla couldn't read her tone. "They are not part of the many," she whispered.

"How can it be?" he asked, sounding more like the lost child.

"Mother can sense it. She can feel the lack of Rohen."

"It is why she was of use before, in helping to find the containment. This is not containment. This is something else."

"But it is a block, a dark spot on the hum of the universe," Isla said.

"Please." The Reader reached for her with his other hand, and Isla took it without hesitation. It was soft and warm, and she was reminded of the master. "There are still those missing from our reach."

"Alice," Isla said, closing her eyes. It was almost as though she could feel her, see her in the darkness behind her lids, and yet she couldn't reach her. Couldn't find her. "Solon," she tried, searching for him, but there was nothing.

"She worked with him," Khalia whispered, her hand tight around Isla's, and there he was, lost in the dark.

"Who are the missing children?" she asked, but it was as though she knew. Their faces appeared in her mind as though she knew them, and yet she hadn't seen them before.

"I don't want to stay here," one of the children in the room with them murmured to another. But they were safe here now. The Rohendra knew where they were.

"We will go to Gray," the minister said, his voice soft and confident.

She felt them move away as one through the Rohen, and Isla looked up at the bent figure of the Reader before her. "Can you see where it isn't?" she asked.

He bowed his head and then shook it. "Take me," he whispered.

Isla was struggling to find the place herself. She stretched out her senses through the hum of the Complex and felt Khalia with her, pushing them further. Then they were in the Rohen, moving through the world and standing in another room. A cottage with nothing but black sky beyond the small window.

Isla turned, releasing her hold on the Reader and Khalia as Alice stood from the small table. She stepped forward, and Isla wrapped her arms around her. The lack of Rohen, the lack of a hum in the surrounding environment, made her heart ache. The Reader groaned. He stepped forward and placed a hand against the wall. And with a rush, the world shifted. The cottage disappeared, and a cave became clear around them. Where the window had looked out at a dark night, the opening of the cave looked over a desolate valley, the night sky wide. Isla stepped forward to take in the beauty of it.

"Where are the children?" she asked, turning back to the woman standing in the middle of the cave. Alice looked tired, her hair messy, her clothing dirty.

"Sleeping," she said, her voice dry as she pointed out two children curled at the back of the cavern.

Khalia walked back through the cave, and Isla followed, worried that she too would disappear again. She squatted down between the children—lying too still, it appeared to Isla. She touched them, whispered something Isla couldn't hear, and they were gone. Then she turned to Alice. "It is time to return to your father," she said. "I will send you to mine."

Isla felt her eyebrows rise. Khalia had never referred to Gray as her father, and she wondered now if that was who she meant. The child reached out and took Alice's hand, and they were gone.

Isla had a moment of panic, that Khalia had again disappeared, but she knew she was safe and had indeed returned to Gray. She could feel the comfort in the Rohen that surrounded her.

"Who is involved in this?" she asked.

"It no longer matters. They are part of the many."

"But are they part of the one?" she asked.

"They have been found," the Reader whispered, and her skin tingled with the sound.

"Will this occur again?"

"That is an odd question," he said.

"Is it? You have foreseen so much, and yet this was something you didn't. Something that escaped your notice even when it was happening, and you don't know for how long."

He bowed his head. "Tevia had slipped through the Rohen. She was lost to what she wanted to be rather than embracing what she was."

"Is it possible other hummers might do the same?" Isla asked.

"It is not possible. I think your queen might sense when there are those disgruntled."

"You have seen more," Isla said.

She could feel his soft smile despite it being lost to the depths of the hood. She understood the Rohen might have lost some to the dark spots in the hum of the universe, but she was sure it wouldn't happen again. "Tevia," she said, unsure if it was a question. What would happen to the girl now that she was no longer connected to the Rohen?

"She is as she should have been. Her mother will care for her as mothers should."

Isla smiled in return then, thankful that the Rohendra had given her this chance to be a mother despite the overwhelming responsibility she felt at times. Perhaps all mothers felt the same, whether their child was Hendra or Queen or something else.

"Where is Solon?" she asked.

The Reader surprised her by shaking his head. She opened her mouth to ask what might happen next, but if they couldn't find him then it would be something else. A bigger question than just where an uncle might have disappeared to. He was the chief of a planet, a council member of the Hendra. Would his son step up—a child himself?

"Should he be found?" the Reader asked.

"I would rather there were not lost places within the Complex, no matter who might be hidden away within them. Are we sure there is no one else who might have been taken or lost within these places?"

The Reader stood motionless for too long. Isla wondered if he was listening to her or seeking out what she hadn't been able to see. "The Rohendra have no secrets. They understand the Complex and all that it holds. We are one and we are many," he whispered, the sound calming as it hummed across her skin.

"Those who returned to the one have shared what was hidden," she said, understanding the Rohendra were one once more.

He bowed his head.

"And what should happen to the uncle?" she asked.

"That is for the niece to decide." He held out a hand, and Solon appeared in the room, leaning back against the wall with his arm across his face to shield his eyes from the dim light. Isla wondered if he too had been kept in the dark.

He groaned and slipped down the wall to lie on the floor, his face still covered. Isla took a deep breath and stepped towards him, resting her hand on his shoulder. He flinched beneath her hold, and then they were in the

Hendra's office, and Gray was throwing his arms around her, murmuring in her ear and holding her far too tightly.

# Epilogue

I sla nestled into Gray's arms on the couch that filled the walls of the private lounge off the office of the Hendra. It was a space they hadn't really utilised, and now it was filled. Khalia sat by her side, the three of them pressed against each other. Across from them were the minister, Alice and several of the children. Some of the very little ones were sleeping in a spare room just along the corridor. The older boy, Damond, sat on the floor leaning against the cushions, his gaze never leaving Khalia.

"Where did he go?" Alice asked.

"Solon has returned home, although he may not be well enough to continue as Chief," Khalia returned. "He has had an ordeal."

"One of his own making," Gray murmured.

"He is to talk to the family about a council member and what is to be done with the planet."

"His wife might take on the role," Alice suggested.

"Or the son," Damond said.

"He might be too young, and I'm not sure what influence the Rohen—Tevia's Rohen—had on him."

"He is at least twice your age," Damond said, looking surprised by her response.

"And yet he has only lived once," Khalia said. Although Isla couldn't see her face clearly, she thought the child poked her tongue out at the boy.

"You have lived before?" Gray asked, a note of fear in his voice.

"I am mostly Rohendra, or part Rohendra; I have lived forever," she said, looking up at him as though he should have understood that without her explaining it.

"And you shall be everlasting," Damond whispered.

She smiled then and leaned back into Isla.

"Would Tevia like to attend our school?" Alice asked.

"I think she has lost any gift she had," Isla murmured, wondering how the Rohendra had removed their essence from her and what was left of the child she had seen disappear into walls.

"When do we return?" Damond asked. Isla felt Khalia stiffen in her arms.

"When it is time. There is much for us to do to help the Hendra first."

Isla was grateful for so many who could support them, support Khalia to be the queen the Rohendra had hoped she would be.

# Acknowledgements

The team at Deranged Doctor Designs (DDD) for absolutely brilliant cover design work and all the marketing extras. Thank you for your support and clear emails around what was needed from me to make the magic happen.

Allison E Wright for wonderful editing work to make my sentences smoother and my intentions clearer.

Special thanks to Yasmin, for taking the time to read my draft and providing ideas to make the story stronger. The support of the Tasmanian Indie Author community and my writerly friends for listening and assisting with all things writing, particularly Danielle, Tara, Nicole, Phyl and Matt.

My parents, Francine and Ken Smith. Amazing, supportive people who I don't thank often enough. Thanks for keeping me grounded and being the best grandparents ever.

As always, Temwa for being my biggest supporter.

# About the Author

Georgina Makalani survives life as a servant of the public by hiding in her office at lunch time with dragons, witches, a laptop and a little bit of magic.

For more about Georgina and her books visit her website: www.theflowofink.com